ALCHEMY AND ARSON

MAGIC & MYSTERY BOOK THREE

LILY WEBB

Print ISBN: 9781799075288

fanmail@lilywebbmysteries.com

www.lilywebbmysteries.com

facebook.com/lilywebbmysteries

twitter.com/lilywebbmystery

instagram.com/lilywebbmysteries

pinterest.com/lilywebbmysteries

goodreads.com/lilywebbmysteries

bookbub.com/authors/lily-webb

amazon.com/author/lilywebb

PREVIOUSLY IN MOON GROVE...

SPELLBOOKS AND STAKINGS RE-CAP

After solving several paranormal murder cases thanks to her telepathic powers, reporter Zoe Clarke was invited to attend school at Veilside Academy of Magic.

But on her first night in school, one of Zoe's professors was staked in her own office and Zoe felt responsible to find the killer.

Thanks to the critical help of a classmate and fast friend, Zoe tracked down the killer and made sure they would never be able to hurt someone again — but Zoe isn't in the clear yet.

Now, expectations of Zoe in Moon Grove and back at home are astronomical. Feeling the pressure, Zoe's longing for the comforts of her old life…

… And her two very different, very separate worlds are about to collide.

Though each book in the Magic & Mystery series can be read alone, the series stands stronger when read together.

If you haven't yet read the first two books in the series, they're available everywhere now!

ALCHEMY AND ARSON

MAGIC & MYSTERY BOOK THREE

CHAPTER ONE

ALL TWELVE MEMBERS of the Moon Grove Council stared down at me from their high-backed chairs on a raised dais, each of them wearing a serious face — if I said having some of the most powerful witches and warlocks in the world scrutinizing me wasn't nerve-wracking, it would've been the understatement of the century.

"Zoe Clarke, at your request, you've come before the eighty-sixth Council of Moon Grove," Heath Highmore, the Head Warlock, said with a warm smile. His salt and pepper hair glimmered in the sun streaming from the skylights above.

"What is it you'd like to speak to us about?" Heath asked.

I drummed my fingers against the table, unable to find words, which was a rarity. Why couldn't the Council have allowed someone to come up to the stand with me?

All I could do was stare at the empty seat next to Heath, the one that'd been vacant for more than a month since the previous Head Witch died. A lot had happened in Moon Grove since then, and not all of it was good.

Circe Woods, Councilwoman and one of my earliest friends in Moon Grove, caught my eyes and smiled at me.

"Zoe, dear, there's no need to be afraid," she said in a motherly tone. "We're here to serve you. You're a citizen of Moon Grove now just like the rest of us, so please, tell us your concerns."

"I-I know, I'm sorry. I'm just nervous," I said and slipped my hands under the table to wipe my sweat-slicked palms on my robes. Though I'd done nothing wrong, I felt like I'd been put on trial —

and after I asked what I needed to, the rest of Moon Grove might wish I had been.

"We understand," Heath said. "Take your time."

"But don't take too long," a beautiful witch with flowing blonde hair at the left end of the row said, her face stern. "You aren't the only witch we're scheduled to hear from today."

She could only be Lorelei Riddle — the mother of Aurelia, who I'd recently gotten thrown in jail for murdering a teacher. I gulped at that realization. How on earth did I keep getting myself into these situations?

"Right, of course," I said. I closed my eyes and took a deep, ragged breath to still my hammering heart. My Grandma Elle's warm southern smile swam into my mind and the image gave me the courage to speak. Everything I was about to do was for her.

I cleared my throat and looked Heath square in the eyes.

"I came before you all today to ask a favor," I said. "A very big one."

The witches and warlocks of the Council exchanged curious looks. It probably wasn't every day that an average citizen asked their elected representatives for a favor, but then again I wasn't exactly average.

"What sort of favor might that be?" Heath asked.

"I know I'm the first outsider to be permitted into Moon Grove in a long time," I started — and froze.

"That's true. Go on," Circe encouraged me, still smiling. Did she already know what I wanted to ask?

"Well, I don't mean to wave my own wand or anything, but I think it's safe to say none of you regrets the decision to allow me in, right?" I asked.

Heath chuckled.

"I'm not so sure the families of those you've put behind bars in the short time you've been here would agree with that assessment, but I think I can speak for the majority of the Council when I say we made the right decision," Heath said.

Lorelei Riddle glared at me, and though I did everything I could to avoid her gaze, I felt it burning on my face. Oh, if looks could kill…

"What are you getting at, Zoe?" Heath asked.

"Well, it's been awfully lonely for me since I got here. I had to leave my whole family behind," I said, and Heath's eyebrows crept up his forehead as he realized what I was trying to say.

"I see," he said as he linked his fingers together under his chin. My heart rate doubled.

"So I was wondering if it might be okay for me to invite my grandmother here for a short visit," I said as fast as I could — like it would take the shock out of the request.

No one said a word, and the deafening silence in the Town Hall was as telling as a collective gasp would've been. I felt like I'd farted at a funeral and everyone knew I was guilty.

Heath straightened in his chair.

"Zoe, while I can appreciate your loneliness, given everything that's gone on in town lately, I'm not sure this is the best time for visitors of any sort, magical or not," Heath said.

Though I'd expected the response, his words still socked me in the gut.

"Is there really such a thing as the best time?" Circe asked, and my heart jumped into my throat where it lodged and continued to pound.

"That's a fair point," Heath said.

"Don't you think Zoe has proven herself trustworthy? This is a small repayment for all the service she's done for Moon Grove," Circe said.

"Agreed," Grace Magnus, who'd only recently returned to work after a vampire attack, said from the right side of the dais. She beamed down at me.

"I owe Ms. Clarke my life. Nothing would make me happier than to welcome her family into Moon Grove," Grace said.

"And let's not forget there's an excellent chance her family members are magical as well. We might miss an exceedingly rare opportunity to learn more about all witches as a group if we denied Zoe's request," Circe said directly to Heath. If I could've hugged her, I would've.

"Yes, but only if what your sister learned about Zoe descending from Lilith is true, which we've yet to verify," Heath said. "Regardless, I still don't think now is the best time. There are big things underway."

"What things?" I interrupted, and again the chamber fell silent. Heath smiled at me, his eyes twinkling as if he were amused, and my face caught fire. Open mouth, insert foot.

"Oh, I'm sure you'll find out soon enough, Ms. Clarke. Nothing seems to slip past you and the rest of the staff at The Messenger," Heath said.

What did that mean? No one at the Moon Grove Messenger had anything at all interesting to report on lately. They obviously knew something we didn't, and I didn't know how to feel about that. Surprises from the Council were rarely good.

"Or perhaps Grave Times beat you to the scoop?" Heath asked. He had to be referring to the new vampire-run and vampire-staffed publication in town — and our biggest upstart competitor.

"It's just my grandma who I'd like to have for a visit. It's not like I'm trying to move my entire family here or anything," I said.

"I understand. Regardless, I think it's time we took a vote on your request," Heath said. He glanced up and down the row at his fellow witches and warlocks. "All those in favor of permitting Zoe's family to visit, raise your wands and say, 'aye.'"

Circe and Grace raised their wands, but no one else did. My heart dropped into my stomach.

"And all those opposed to the request, raise your wands and say, 'nay,'" Heath said. Ten wands shot into the air along with their owners' voices, all denying me. Heath gave me a soft, sad smile and rested his hands on the table.

Lorelei, however, looked absolutely triumphant as she stared down her nose at me from the dais. Maybe she felt like she'd gotten back at me for getting her daughter arrested. I didn't have the spirit left to figure it out nor care.

"I'm sorry, dear, but the Council has voted not to approve a visit at this time. However, feel free to try again later when circumstances are less, well, unsettled," Heath said.

I could only assume he was referring to all the trouble that'd gone on in Moon Grove lately — much of it made worse by my intervention.

"Right, yeah, okay. Can I, uh, can I go then?" I asked.

"If you have no other questions or concerns, of course," Heath said. He was trying to be nice, which I appreciated, but all I wanted was to get out of the Town Hall and as far away from the Council as possible.

"No, that's everything, thanks for hearing me out," I said — though I'd gotten nothing out of it other than a mild case of depression.

"Then this meeting is adjourned," Heath said. "The Council will break for five minutes before we move on to the next guest."

I shoved back from the table, slung my bag over my shoulder, and tried my best not to meet eyes with any of the dozens of people who'd gathered to listen as I made a beeline for the door. Somehow, I doubted Lorelei was the only one happy to see me not get what I wanted for once.

A hand on my shoulder jolted me out of my racing thoughts and I whirled to find Circe smiling at me.

"Can we talk?" she asked, her loose auburn bun threatening to tumble off her head as she jerked it toward the hall that held her office.

"Sure," I said with a shrug. She led me into her space and I was surprised by how small and cramped it was, due in no small part to the amount of clutter that littered every free inch of surface area.

"I'd offer you a place to sit, but one's not readily available and this won't take long anyway," Circe said as she sat on the one corner of her desk that poked out from under papers and file folders.

"Listen, I know you're disappointed about the Council's ruling, but don't get discouraged," Circe said.

"Why shouldn't I?"

"Well, I can't say anything about it officially just yet, but I think if you're unhappy with the Council's ruling, maybe you should consider throwing your name in the ring as someone who might be able to change things around here," Circe said.

"Wait, are you saying what I think you are?" I whispered as if anyone but her would hear me anyway. "Is that what Heath meant when he said big things are underway?"

Circe smiled and nodded. "You didn't honestly think we'd leave the Head Witch position vacant forever, did you?"

"No, of course not, but so soon? And with all this other stuff that's been going on lately?" I asked.

"That's exactly why the Council feels we need to fill the position," Circe said.

"Wait, am I allowed to report on this? Can I quote you anonymously?" I asked.

"No, I'm sorry," Circe said. I groaned and Circe laughed. "But don't worry, there should be an official announcement very soon."

"Any insider info as to who's going to run?" I asked.

"I have a few ideas, but no one's announced yet given that there's not officially an election on the calendar," Circe said.

Maybe it was a good thing the Council had ruled not to let Grandma Elle come to town after all. I couldn't imagine trying to host her while something like a Head Witch election was happening. It would've been chaos, even for Moon Grove.

"I think you should consider it, Zoe," Circe said.

"Are you serious?"

"Why wouldn't I be? You've done a lot for this town and people love you," Circe said.

"I dunno about that. Did you see the way Lorelei was looking at me? Somehow, I doubt she'd be thrilled to support me," I said.

"You don't need to win everyone over in order to win the election," Circe said.

She had a point.

"This is nuts. I've only been here, what, a little more than a month? There are plenty of better-qualified witches in town than me. For Lilith's sake, I don't even know how to use this thing," I said as I drew my wand from my robes, which I'd had for just about a week.

Circe pushed my wand away from her face.

"Well, the first rule, never point your wand at someone unless you intend to use it, dear," Circe said, smiling.

"Sorry," I said and pocketed it again before I put someone's eye out — or turned them into a frog.

"In any case, I'm sure Raina would be happy to take you on for lessons again if you did decide to run," Circe said.

"Your sister's done more than enough favors for me, I couldn't ask her for another," I said. Had it not been for the Headmistress of the Veilside Academy of Magic, I wouldn't even have a wand in the first place.

"You don't have to decide now. Take some time to think about it. Of course, I'll support your run if it comes to that," Circe said, her smile widening. "Anyway, we'd better get back out there before anyone starts suspecting things."

She stood and led me back out into the hall, which was full of noise as people shuffled their bodies and chairs.

"Thanks for the heads up," I said.

"Anytime," Circe said, and I took the opportunity to leave before anyone else had a chance to stop me. Outside, the fresh air was barely enough to keep me from floating away in my thoughts again.

I needed to call Grandma Elle to tell her the bad news before I went back to the office, but the thought of actually doing it made my skin crawl. Elle was so excited to come and see me, my friends, and my new life in Moon Grove — and now I had to call her and ruin it.

The Council must've had their reasons for voting against me, but it still made me feel like I'd overestimated how highly they thought of me.

I dug my phone out of my bag and tapped to Grandma Elle's contact card. My finger hovered over the "call" button. What could I say? Elle knew her visit was subject to the Council's approval, so she'd probably understand, but I knew she'd be crushed.

She wasn't the only one.

Sighing, I tapped the call button and held the phone to my ear but barely heard the ring over the whooshing of anxious blood pumping in my veins.

"Hey, Sugar," Grandma answered, her accent sweeter than apple pie and, as usual, I could see the smile on her face in my mind. The image was bittersweet.

"Hey, Gram."

"I reckon you're callin' cuz you've got good news fer me?" Grandma asked.

My voice caught in my throat like grits.

"Sugar? You there?"

"Yes and no," I said when I found my tongue again.

"What's that mean? You're either there or you ain't."

"No, I meant I have good and bad news. I went in front of the Council just now like I said I was going to, so that's the good news," I said. The line went silent for a few moments, interrupted only by the crackle of static.

"And the bad news?" Grandma asked. My heart hammered in the back of my throat like it was trying to climb its way out of me, and I couldn't bring myself to say it. My phone slipped down my ear thanks to the sweat on my palm.

"Just kidding, there isn't any bad news, you're welcome to come," I said, hating myself as soon as the lie slipped out of my mouth — which had turned so dry it hurt to speak.

"Really?!" Grandma shouted. "Oh my Lord, Zoe, that's great news! I'm so excited! When should I make my way over?"

"I can get you on a bus here tomorrow," I said, unable to believe myself as I kept the lie going. But what was I supposed to do? I'd already told Gram she could come and if I admitted I'd been lying, she'd never forgive me.

Then again, there wasn't any way to hide the truth if and when she got here.

"Are you sure? That seems awful quick," Grandma said.

"I'm sure, Gram," I said, not at all sure.

I'd just have to figure it all out when she got here. Maybe once the Council got to know her they'd know Grandma wasn't any risk at all. Besides, between all the people I'd helped them lock up for murder and all the residents I'd saved as a result, they owed me a favor.

"I'll book the ticket for you when I get home from work in a bit," I said, making a mental note to ask Flora, my fairy roommate and co-worker who'd no doubt be upset with me for lying, to help me get a seat on the Silver Bullet bus for Gram. As for where Elle would sleep, well, I'd have to figure that out later too.

"I can't wait to see you, Sugar. You wouldn't believe me if I told ya how much I've missed you and that little black varmint cat of yours," Grandma said.

"We've missed you too, Gram. The farm's boring enough when we're there, I can't imagine how mind-numbing it must be without us to entertain you," I said.

"I'm gonna pretend I didn't hear that young lady," Grandma said and I laughed, realizing how badly I wanted to see her. "Anywho, I reckon I better light a fire under this old rump and start packin' or I ain't never gonna get there."

"Okay. Just make sure you're at the Lumberton bus station first thing in the morning and look out for a big silver bus. You'll know it when you see it," I said.

"Does that mean it's gonna be packed full of Pagans?" Grandma asked and I laughed.

"What is it with you and the Pagans, anyway?"

"I'll take that as a yes," Grandma sighed. "Guess that means I need to make sure I pack as many crosses as I can."

"Whatever helps you sleep, Gram," I said. "Listen, I need to get back to work. I'll email you the ticket to print out later. Let me know if you run into any hiccups."

"Zoe, Sugar, I'm about to board a bus goin' to a town full of witches, psychics, and Lord only knows what other dark-sided deviants. There's darn sure gonna be hiccups," Grandma said.

"I know. Just take it easy, say an extra prayer tonight if you think it'll help," I said.

"You can bet yer keister I will," Grandma said.

"Good. I love you, Gram. Talk to you tomorrow."

"Love you too," Grandma said and clicked off the line.

I stood staring at my phone knowing I'd made a terrible mistake and that I couldn't take it back now.

But even if I could, I wouldn't have. I was going to see Grandma Elle and that was all that mattered.

CHAPTER TWO

I STUMBLED through the front doors of the Moon Grove Messenger the next day looking like a zombie who'd stuck a fork in a toaster. Luckily, Flora was the first person to spot me.

"Dear Lilith, what happened to you?" she hissed as her four fluttering wings carried her around desks and magically flying objects to me.

"I had trouble falling asleep last night and slept through my alarm," I said.

"Why couldn't you sleep?"

"Reasons," I mumbled, looking away from her.

"And what reasons might those be?" she asked. I'd already told her everything about how my request to the Council went after work last night, so of course, she saw right through me.

"The kind I'm not going to tell you about," I said.

"Why not?"

"Because it doesn't matter," I said.

Of all people, I could've trusted Flora with the truth, but I didn't feel like having that conversation right now. I'd been up all night thinking about it anyway so I didn't want to give the issue any more real estate in my brain.

"Okay, if you say so," Flora said, looking me up and down like a wild animal that might lash out at her at any second.

"I do need you to do me a favor, though," I said. Slowly, my eyes crept up to meet hers and she raised one eyebrow at me.

"You asking for favors never pans out well," she said. Yeah, I'd learned that the hard way thanks to the Council.

"Well, you probably won't feel any different once I ask you," I said.

"Let's at least go to my desk, everyone is staring at us," she said, and without waiting for my response she took me by the arm and pulled me through the office. It took everything I had not to look up, but I could feel all the eyes on me anyway.

I didn't have to be a rocket scientist to figure out that a roomful of journalists had probably already heard about my meeting with the Council. Lilith only knew what they would think when they found out I was about to smuggle my grandmother into town against the Council's orders.

Flora sat down at her desk and motioned for me to sit too. I parked on the corner and searched my brain for words, which seemed all jumbled up in my head.

"Before I agree to anything, you have to tell me what it is," Flora said as she pushed a strand of her silver-blonde hair behind one of her pointed ears.

"It's no big deal, I just want you to book a ticket for somebody on the Silver Bullet bus," I said. Flora eyed me suspiciously.

"The only reason you'd have to book a ticket on that is if you were trying to leave Moon Grove," she said. "Are you going on a vacation you haven't told me about?"

"It's not for me," I said, and Flora's eyes went wide.

"Then who is it for?"

"A friend."

"Zoe, please tell me you're not doing what I think you're doing," Flora said.

"Have I ever been known to follow the rules?" I asked and Flora frowned at me.

"I don't like this at all. Are you really going to defy the Council?"

"It wouldn't be the first time, would it?" I asked.

"No, I guess not. When do you need a ticket?" Flora asked, her fingers already gliding across her keyboard.

"Tonight, preferably with a late arrival," I said. Flora sighed.

"You owe me big time, you know that, right?" Flora asked.

"Oh, trust me, I'm well aware. Forward me the details when you get them so I can pass them on to the passenger," I said, careful not to use Grandma's name in the office. There was no telling who was listening or what they might do with the information.

"Is Mitch here yet?" I asked.

"I didn't see him come in, but I'm pretty sure he's in his office," Flora said.

"Good. I have some things I need to talk to him about," I said and pushed off Flora's desk and heading for the Editor-in-Chief's office.

The door was already cracked open so I knocked on the frame.

"Come in," Mitch called, his voice deep and growly. I shoved the door open and stepped inside like a child about to be apprehended by the principal at school.

"Hey, good morning, Zoe. What's going on?" Mitch asked. I closed the door behind me and the smile Mitch wore faded fast.

"I have some stuff I want to ask you about if that's okay?" I asked.

"Of course. What's on your mind?"

"It's about the Council," I said.

"I'm listening," Mitch said, encouragingly. "What about them?"

"Well, Councilwoman Woods pulled me aside afterward and told me some interesting rumors," I said.

"Like what?"

"I don't know for sure, but it sounds like there's going to be another election for Head Witch soon," I said.

Mitch crossed his arms over his chest and sat back in his chair, which creaked under his shifting weight. He was a huge guy, and nearly every inch of him was covered in hair — not unusual for a werewolf.

"A new election, is that right?" he asked. "Are you sure? That seems awfully soon after the last one."

"Yeah, that's exactly what I said. So I take it you haven't heard any rumblings about this yet?" I asked.

"None at all," he said with a shrug. "But it's funny you should say this because I heard some other stuff."

"What other stuff?"

"When I got into the office this morning there was a memo from the Council on my desk. Evidently, they're holding another meeting today to make some sort of major announcement, but they didn't say what it was about," Mitch said.

"Do you have any guesses?"

"Honestly, not a single one. Trying to predict what they're up to these days is like trying to guess the weather," Mitch said.

"Good thing the Council is my beat," I said.

"It is, but are you sure it's a good idea for you to cover it based on everything else going on? It looks like you had a rough night," Mitch said.

"I did, but I'm going anyway. There's nothing a strong cup of MagiJava can't cure," I said.

"That's my girl," Mitch said, smiling.

"When's the meeting?"

"10 o'clock," Mitch said. My heart skipped a beat. That was in less than twenty minutes — yeah, I was *that* late for work.

"Guess I'd better go get ready then," I said.

"Good luck. Let me know if there's anything I can help with," Mitch said.

I left and walked to my own desk to gather my things — a pad of paper and something to write with, old school — and was just heading out the door when Flora called to me.

"Zoe!"

"What is it?" I called without looking back.

"Check your phone, I got you what you needed," Flora said.

I waved at her over my shoulder and headed outside, the blast of cold morning air in my face jarring. It took a few moments for me to get my bearings, and I was thankful I was only walking across the street. I didn't think I could've made it much further than that.

I crossed Luna Street and walked through the giant double doors of the Town Hall to find it absolutely overflowing with people from all different walks of life: witches, warlocks, werewolves, even vampires — in broad daylight.

Whatever the Council was about to announce, it was going to be big. Why else would literally everyone in Moon Grove have gathered to hear about it?

There were so many people milling about talking to each other that it was difficult to walk through the narrow aisles separating the rows of chairs that fanned from the dais.

I forced my way to the front of the room and smiled when I saw Beau Duncan, my boyfriend and lead anchor for Moon Grove's Channel 666, standing in front of a video camera waiting to broadcast, a microphone held in one hand.

A young-looking vampire I didn't recognize stood idly chatting with Beau, whose curly black hair dangled to one side of his face. He pushed his speckled brown glasses up his nose and fiddled with the expensive, fancy looking camera wrapped around his neck. Did vampires even need glasses, or were they just for looks?

It struck me that I'd never seen Beau at work, but watching him network only made him cuter than he already was.

Beau spotted me as I approached. He excused himself and set his microphone on the nearest chair to smile and throw his arms open to me. His warm brown eyes and perfect smile sparkled and instantly made me feel better.

"There she is! I was starting to worry you were going to miss the big news, and Lilith knows that's not like you," Beau said, wrapping his arms tight around me as we met.

"Sorry to interrupt, Mr…?" I asked as Beau released me, and offered my hand for a shake.

"Desfleurs. Marcel Desfleurs," the vampire said as he slipped his frigid right hand into mine. His blood-red pupils pierced right through me as he stared into my eyes. Between his gaze and his subzero body temperature, it was a struggle to fight back the shudder I felt building inside.

"Nice to meet you. I'm—"

"Zoe Clarke, yes, I'm well aware," Marcel interrupted, an unsettling smile spreading across his face. "Everyone at Grave Times knows who you are. Your reputation precedes you, Ms. Clarke."

"So I take it that means you're an employee?" I asked. Smiling wider, Marcel flashed me the press badge hanging around his neck, concealed by his camera. Sure enough, it read, "Marcel Desfleurs, Photographer, Grave Times."

"You catch every little detail, don't you?" Marcel asked, one side of his mouth curled in a smile.

"A vampire photographer? Now that's funny. Is your staff photo just a blank circle?" I fired back and Beau choked.

"I was just chatting with Marcel about his new paper," Beau said, trying to smooth things over. "It's so new."

"That's right. It's only about a week old," Marcel said.

"Which is like, what, a blink of an eye for a vampire?" I asked. Beau blushed and Marcel smirked.

"Give or take," he said.

"Well, I think it's good to have as much representation in the media as possible," Beau said. "So I'm glad to see the vampires branching out."

"Agreed. Our main motivation with Grave Times is to present life in Moon Grove as we vampires see and experience it," Marcel said.

As noble as he made it seem, it sounded like a load of troll poo to me. I'd just opened my mouth to tell Marcel that when the thunderous sound of the Head Warlock's gavel rang throughout the hall.

"Please take your seats, everyone, we'd like to begin," Heath Highmore's disembodied voice said, magically amplified to fill the entire space. Right on cue, the twelve members of the Council appeared from thin air in their seats on the raised dais — except for Heath, who stood.

Rustling filled the hall as everyone struggled to sit and arrange their things. I plopped down next to Beau, my pen and paper at the ready. There was no telling what the Council was about to announce, but I didn't want to miss it.

"Before we get started, for the sake of everyone's comfort, the Council respectfully requests that any questions be saved until after the meeting is adjourned," Heath said.

A mumble of agreement carried through the hall.

"Good. Now, as I'm sure you're all aware, tonight is set to be a very special evening," Heath said. Excited whispers flared up among the crowd, but I didn't have any idea what they were so excited about.

"A full moon is a challenging event for us each time it arrives in Moon Grove," Heath said. "But tonight we're preparing for a full moon unlike the others; tonight the Blood Moon rises."

A collective gasp tore through the attendees. The Blood Moon? Was that a bad thing? As far as I knew that was just a kind of eclipse. Sometimes being the new kid on the magical block wasn't ideal.

"Why's that special?" I whispered in Beau's ear, but he shushed me.

"The Blood Moon presents particular challenges and affects us all. Unfortunately, beyond the werewolves, we haven't yet determined exactly what those effects could be," Heath said.

That didn't sound good, but it explained why the Council had refused to let Grandma Elle come to town. The full moon turned werewolves into their wolf forms, and I hadn't yet seen exactly what that meant for everyone else in Moon Grove.

"I have much more to say on this matter, but before I do, let me introduce you all to a special witch, Ms. Hilda Blackwood," Heath said, gesturing to his left.

A witch with wild silver hair held off her forehead by a lime green headband stumbled out in front of the dais. She wore glasses so thick they amplified her beady eyes to three times their size, and a royal purple shawl hung from her bony shoulders. Her forearms were covered in beads of various sizes and colors that she couldn't stop herself from fingering.

If I didn't know any better I would've sworn she was on something.

"Beyond being the owner of the new alchemical shop Hypnotic Tonics, Ms. Blackwood is a gifted Seer," Heath said. "We've asked her to use her abilities to predict what we might see tonight. Ms. Blackwood?"

Hilda nodded and closed her eyes as she toyed with her beads. For what seemed like forever, nothing happened — until Hilda's eyes snapped open to reveal nothing but milky white. A chill tore through the room, extinguishing the candles that lined the Council's dais, and I shuddered.

"Death," Hilda rattled, her voice faint. "This Blood Moon will bring death."

No one said a word.

"How? To whom?" Heath whispered, but Hilda's vision seemed to have passed. Her eyes fluttered and she might've fallen if someone in the front row hadn't rushed to catch her.

Heath and the rest of the Council members exchanged concerned looks. Clearly, this wasn't what they'd expected when they asked Hilda to make a prediction. Normally, I wouldn't have paid any attention to a fortune teller, but that was outside Moon Grove. Everything here was different.

The man who'd caught Hilda helped her walk away, and Heath cleared his throat.

"I apologize for the rather disturbing display. It wasn't our intention to frighten any of you," Heath said. "That said, I think we have no choice but to impose a curfew this evening for everyone's safety. It's anyone's guess what the Blood Moon could do."

A curfew? For tonight? Great. Awesome. Fantastic. It wasn't like I was planning to sneak an outsider into town or anything. Life just kept getting better.

"This is outrageous!" a gruff voice shouted from somewhere toward the back of the room, startling me. I whirled around to find a bald, burly man in a leather jacket standing and jabbing a tattooed finger through the air at Heath.

"You wouldn't do this to the vampires who we all know are more dangerous, so why are you punishing us werewolves like this?!" the man shouted.

"Please, Mr. Romano, calm down," Heath said. "I assure you, this is for everyone's safety. Many magical species are affected by the Blood Moon, not merely werewolves."

"Don't tell me to calm down! We don't even have anyone up there representing us or who knows a thing about what it's like to be a werewolf on a full moon and that's clearly what this is all about! You witches are just afraid of what you don't understand!" the man continued, and in seconds the gargoyles who served as the Council's guards were on him.

The man kicked and snarled as the gargoyles seized him, but he was no match for their strength. It happened in a flash, but I could've sworn I saw the man's teeth sharpen and lengthen, and for a second I wondered if Heath was right to impose a curfew. The gargoyles dragged him through the Town Hall's doors and that was the last I saw of Mr. Romano.

"Please don't be alarmed," Heath said, though he looked shaken himself. "We must remain calm. So long as everyone follows the rules, we'll all be safe and this night will pass uneventfully just like the rest."

Even I had trouble believing that. There was no such thing as an uneventful night in Moon Grove.

"To that end, effective immediately, all citizens must be indoors by eight o'clock this evening. Patrols will make their rounds to ensure compliance and anyone caught in violation will be detained. Further, all evening activities, including classes at Veilside, are suspended until further notice," Heath said.

Wait, patrols? Wasn't the police force made up of werewolves? If they were at risk of turning into killing machines with no control over themselves then who was going to keep the rest of us safe and how?

More importantly, how was I supposed to sneak Elle into town without getting both of us torn to shreds by a rogue, rabid werewolf — or worse?

At least school was canceled, right?

CHAPTER THREE

MIDNIGHT COULDN'T COME FAST ENOUGH. Flora had gone to bed long ago and Luna, my talking black cat, had thankfully joined her.

But I couldn't have slept even if I'd tried. All I could think about was Grandma Elle and how on Earth I was supposed to get her into Moon Grove without anyone seeing us — and without either of us getting mauled.

Instead, I sat on the couch in the living room for hours staring out the window at Flora's immaculately decorated garden and Moon Grove beyond it, my mind racing. Everything was bathed in a creepy red light from the Blood Moon.

The clock hanging above the entrance to the kitchen ticked away the seconds torturously. Elle's bus was scheduled to arrive at the Moon Grove town gates in less than half an hour and I still hadn't formulated a plan.

"Zoe?" Flora asked, jolting me. She stood in the doorway to her bedroom holding Luna against her chest. "Are you okay?"

"Yeah, I'm fine. I just can't sleep," I muttered.

"I don't need fairy intuition to know that's a lie," Flora said as she came to sit next to me. Luna crawled into my lap.

"She's right. You've never been a good liar," Luna said.

"And you've never been one to pull punches," I said, and Flora laughed.

"What can I say, I call things as I see them," Luna said as she licked a paw and dragged it over the top of her head.

"I take it this has to do with your grandmother?" Flora asked.

"Yeah, obviously," I sighed. "I have no idea what to do. I mean, I was already in hot water before they decided to implement this curfew. Now I'm totally out of luck."

"I wish there was something I could do to help," Flora said. "But I wouldn't dare step outside tonight."

"I don't blame you. You'd be like a super snack for all the werewolves, vampires, and whatever else is out there looking for dinner," I said.

"Well, regardless, you can't just leave your grandmother alone. What are you going to do?"

"Good question. I don't have a broom to fly on, so I guess I'll have to do things the old-fashioned way," I said. Now more than ever I wished I'd elected to take flying lessons at Veilside.

"What does that mean?"

"Sneaking around in the dark and praying I don't get caught," I said. "Sounds like a pretty foolproof plan, right?"

"Aren't there any spells you could cast on yourself? Something to make you invisible?" Flora asked.

"Are you kidding? Even if there was, do you really think I could pull it off?" I asked as I pulled my wand out of my robes. There was something almost cruel about having a wand and not knowing how to use it. It was like giving a kid a Tolstoy novel.

"Yeah, you might just end up hurting yourself if you tried," Flora sighed.

"Do you really think there's anything dangerous out there? Or do you think the Council was trying to scare people into staying inside just in case?"

"After that disturbing prediction from Hilda, I highly doubt they were just making things up to frighten us," Flora said, and a chill ran down my spine at the memory. As much as I didn't want to believe Flora, I knew she was right.

"Have you looked outside? Everything looks so eerie," I said, pointing out the window. I'd been staring at it for hours so it had mostly lost its impact, but there was no denying something strange was happening. All the bushes and flowers were covered in a blood-red glow.

"I've tried not to, honestly," Flora said. "The less I think about it, the less I have to worry about what's going on out there."

"I don't even understand what the point of the curfew is. How is that going to stop some mooned-up werewolf from barging into someone's house?" I asked.

"I'm trying not to think about that either," Flora groaned.

"Sorry, I wasn't trying to upset you," I said.

"It's okay, I know you weren't. Besides, you've got much more to worry about than I do," Flora said.

"Well, if it's any consolation, I've survived an attack from a murderous vampire, and I managed to keep myself alive when a crazy witch threw me out of a sixth-floor window, so I think I'll be all right," I said.

Flora chuckled. "That's one way to look at it."

"Anyway, I guess I'd better get moving. I don't want Elle to be alone waiting for me. As dangerous as things are inside town tonight, I can't imagine what it's going to be like outside the gates," I said.

"I'm sure I don't need to tell you this, but I'll say it anyway: please be careful, Zoe," Flora said.

"I'll do my best. No promises."

"That's not funny," Flora said as she leaned over to hug me like it was the last time she might have the chance.

I choked up a little bit. We hadn't been roommates for long, but I already felt like she was my best friend in the world.

"At least I know Luna will have a home if I don't make it back," I said, scratching the top of Luna's head.

"That's not funny either," Flora said.

I slipped my wand back into my robes and stood to stare out the window at the bizarre red world that waited for me outside. It felt like I'd taken a rocket ship to Mars. Despite the fact it was almost midnight, the light from the moon was so bright that it seemed like it was nearly noon, not midnight.

But at least this way the werewolves and other creepy crawlies wouldn't have any shadows to hide in.

"Good luck," Flora said as she walked me to the front door. Gulping, I turned the knob and stepped outside slowly, checking both sides to make sure nothing was waiting to grab me.

When I was sure the coast was clear, I nodded to Flora and she closed the door, leaving me all on my own. Somewhere off in the distance, a long, high-pitched wolf's howl tore through the air and brought every hair on my body to attention.

This was crazy, completely crazy. But what choice did I have? I couldn't leave Elle alone at the gates with her luggage and whatever else was out there. The fact of the matter was I created this problem myself — if I'd had the courage to tell Grandma it wasn't the right time to visit, none of this would've happened.

Or the Council could've approved my request.

The thought gave me the resolve to see things through, even if it wasn't one of my better ideas. After all I'd done for the Council and for Moon Grove, the least they could do to repay me was allow Gram to come and visit.

Now they didn't have a choice.

With my head held high, I stepped off down the path and turned left onto Swiftsage. Had it not been for the unsettling color and size of the moon that dominated the sky, and the nightmarish crimson shade it cast over everything, the street would've looked the same as it always did.

Crouching to keep myself as low to the ground as possible — as if that would do anything to make me less conspicuous — I hurried down the street toward the intersection of Crescent and Swiftsage.

Despite what Heath had said about there being patrols to make sure everyone complied with the curfew, I saw no evidence. Maybe even the people hired to patrol were too scared to do it. I wouldn't blame them.

Hugging the brush that lined Crescent Street, I hopped from cluster to cluster moving south toward the town gates. All the myriad shops and businesses that were normally lit up like Christmas trees were as dark inside as ink.

I'd never seen Moon Grove so quiet and it was beyond scary. They say that there are certain cities that never sleep, and Moon Grove was definitely one of them, but even the oil lamps that normally kept the streets bathed in warm light were extinguished.

I tried not to think about what that meant as I crept further south, my eyes and ears strained for any sight or sound of something other than human. At that point, I'd rather have gotten caught by one of the patrols than run into a shifted werewolf — especially after the way I'd seen Mr. Romano change earlier.

Amazingly enough, I managed to make it to the gates without running into anyone or anything, not even an animal. It was almost alarming how easy it was to sneak across town; maybe my luck hadn't run out after all.

As I stood looking out through the open gate — there was no reason to lock it since it was magically protected to prevent anyone non-magical from entering — it occurred to me I wasn't sure I'd be able to get back into town once I left.

The first time I walked through the gates, Beau had dragged me while insisting I must've had some sort of magical blood. But from my perspective, the only thing I saw waiting for me on the other side of the gates was a rundown town.

I strongly suspected Grandma Elle had some magic in her blood as well, but I wasn't sure. What if she couldn't enter the town at all? Then what would I do? I couldn't put her back on the bus and send her home because the bus didn't wait. Even if it did, she would never go for it.

Just like every other part of my plan, it seemed I would have to make it up as I went. If I couldn't get back into town, well, at least Elle wouldn't be alone. And if she couldn't walk through the gates, I would just have to figure something else out.

My palms slick with sweat, and my eyes closed tight, I stepped through the gates and kept walking blindly until I knew I was well past the point of no return.

My eyes fluttered open and I let out a sigh of relief as I realized I was out of the magical bounds of Moon Grove for the first time in more than a month — and I hadn't burst into flames or anything as a result.

The bad news was that Grandma Elle wasn't there yet.

I pulled my phone out of my robes to check the time only to find that, of course, the display was scrambled. In the same way that my human cell phone had gone haywire when I entered Moon Grove, my Paraphone had done the exact same thing upon leaving the magical boundaries of the town.

Hopefully, that would fix itself once we got back inside. It was the least of my concerns.

As if on cue, a sound like gunfire erupted and I shrieked as a gigantic silver bus appeared out of thin air in front of me. The screech of its brakes grated against my eardrums as the bus ground to a halt.

The front door hissed open to reveal a vampire with long, greasy black hair giving me the worst kind of smile. It was Claude, the same vampire who'd driven the bus to Moon Grove when I came.

"Zoe, *ma chérie*, you smell as fresh and delightful as I remember," Claude said from the driver's seat. In the blink of an eye, he was beside me sniffing me like a dog.

"Thanks, Claude," I said, ignoring him to peer into the bus for any sign of Elle. "It's good to see you again too." Nothing could have been further from the truth — Claude was as creepy and weird as ever, unfortunately.

"When a frightened little old lady got on my bus, I knew right away she was related to you," Claude said. "And here she comes."

"Zoe, are you there?" Grandma's voice called from deep inside the bus. Just the sound of it made my heart lurch.

"Yes, Gram! I'm here, get off the bus," I said.

A few moments passed in which I held my breath while I waited. Elle spilled off the bus with nothing but an oversized backpack slung over her shoulders. She recoiled as she passed Claude and threw her arms around me. Tears streamed down her face and wet my shoulder.

"Oh, Sugar, I'm so glad to see you," Grandma sobbed.

"Are you okay? What's wrong?" I asked.

"You mean other than going through H-E-double-hockey-sticks to get here?" Grandma asked. "Good Lord in heaven, Zoe, what ungodly nonsense have you dragged me into?"

"We can talk about it later, we need to get going. Come on," I said, peeling her off me. She nodded and wiped the tears from her eyes.

"Did you bring anything else with you?"

Grandma shook her head.

"I had no idea how long I'd be here or what I'd need or if you could just magic it up fer me or somethin'," Grandma said and I had to bite back a laugh. If she thought I could impress her with magic, she was going to be sorely disappointed.

"Don't worry about it, we can get whatever you need in town," I said, jabbing a finger over my shoulder at the gates.

"You're pullin' my leg ain't you? There ain't nothing back there but busted shacks. Zoe, I rarely take the Lord's name in vain, but I swear to God if you're crankin' my chain with all this Pagan hooplah—"

"I'm not, I swear. You have to believe me, there's more than meets the eye. You'll see soon enough," I said, though I didn't know how true that would be. For all I knew, Grandma might not even be able to enter Moon Grove.

"Regardless, I need you to pull yourself together. Things are a little, well, complicated right now so we need to be clear headed," I said. I'd have to come clean with her about lying at some point, but now clearly wasn't the time.

"Complicated? Is that what y'all witches call this?" Grandma asked.

"Come on, the sooner we get you to my place, the better," I said.

"I hope to the Lord above you've got an ice-cold glass of Southern Comfort waitin' fer me," Grandma sighed. "I reckon I'mma need it."

She wasn't alone. So far I'd managed to get to her without an issue, but sneaking us both back to Flora's house would be another matter entirely.

"*Enchantée*, Madame," Claude cooed as he bowed and practically teleported back into the driver's seat of the bus. "Take care of yourself, Zoe."

"Yeah, you too. Stay out of the sun, it's bad for your skin," I said, and Claude smirked.

I took Grandma's hand in mine and walked toward the open gates, saying a silent prayer that everything would go as I hoped.

"This might feel weird for a second," I warned Grandma. Truthfully, I had no idea what was going to happen, but I had to prepare her somehow.

"Can't be any worse than what I just saw," Grandma said. "Ain't no amount of church-goin' gonna cure me of this."

"You might want to close your eyes," I said.

"Zoe, Sugar, you say that like they ain't been closed the whole time," Grandma said.

With a deep breath and a renewed grip on Elle's hand, I set off at a brisk pace through the gates. Amazingly, as the illusion of a shantytown melted away and the crimson-bathed scenery of the real Moon Grove appeared, nothing happened to Grandma.

We stopped and I waited for Grandma to open her eyes. When she did, she let out a gasp and clapped a hand over her mouth.

"What in the Lord's name…?" she whispered as she looked around. Okay, so that answered that question: Grandma definitely had some sort of magic in her blood because she could see the real town.

But the Blood Moon probably wasn't helping her impression of things. There wasn't anything I could do about that.

"I told you things were complicated right now, but anyway, welcome to Moon Grove," I said, shrugging.

"Zoe, there's someone coming," Grandma said, pointing down Crescent Street. I whirled and saw my entire life flashing before me as Circe Woods came stomping down the street in our direction, her robes flowing, her wand pointed directly at me.

Busted.

"Zoe Clarke, I *do* hope this isn't what it looks like!" Circe hissed as she jogged the rest of the way to me and Grandma, looking over her shoulder to make sure we were alone.

"I reckon you know her?" Grandma whispered, but I shushed her.

"Circe, I know this looks funny, but I swear, I can explain everything if you give me the chance," I said.

"You don't need to explain. It's crystal clear, and we can't have this conversation here."

"Then where can we —"

I never finished the sentence. My whole world turned into a twisted blur of colors and Grandma's shrieks. The next thing I knew, my rear collided with the floor of a dark house I didn't recognize, Grandma next to me. All the drapes were drawn and there wasn't a single light on inside. Grandma clutched my arm and whimpered.

"Where are we?" she whispered.

"I don't know."

Seconds later, Circe appeared in a loud crack. She flung her wand in the direction of a nearby fireplace and it burst to life with flame, making Grandma shout. Pictures of Circe and Raina on the mantle flickered in the light from the fire. Were we at Circe's?

"What on earth were you thinking, Zoe? Are you trying to get yourself thrown out of town, or worse?"

"No, I'm sorry, I don't know what I was thinking, maybe I wasn't thinking at all —"

"Clearly you weren't. Mrs. Clarke, I'm sorry we met this way, but such is life," Circe said to Grandma, who looked completely bewildered. She sat staring at Circe, her mouth opening and closing like a fish out of water.

"She's a little overwhelmed," I said.

"Rightfully so. Zoe, this is unbelievable," Circe said. "What possessed you to go against the Council's wishes?"

"I didn't feel like it was fair as a ruling after all I've done," I said, my face burning as I realized how lame it sounded coming out of my mouth.

"That's childish and you know it. You should thank Lilith herself it was me who found you two and not someone — or some*thing* — else lurking in the darkness," Circe said.

"Now hold on a tootin' minute. Zoe, you *lied* to me?" Grandma asked and I knew I was in serious trouble.

"Well, I'd say it was more a stretch of the truth than a —"

"I've said it before and I'll say it again, where did I go wrong with you, child?" Grandma interrupted, throwing her hands in the air. Despite her anger, Circe smiled.

"Mrs. Clarke, it's not safe in Moon Grove right now for anyone, much less for someone who isn't familiar with magic and the magical world," Circe said. "Under normal circumstances, I'd arrange for you to return home immediately, but that's not possible tonight."

"You mean because of the hour?" Grandma asked. Circe frowned and shook her head.

"No, because of a temporary curfew that's been implemented for everyone's safety," Circe said.

"Safety?" Grandma repeated.

"Yes. Tonight we're experiencing a Blood Moon, which aggravates the conditions of werewolves and makes them much more dangerous," Circe explained.

"*Werewolves?*" Grandma gasped. All the color drained from her face and she looked like she might pass out.

"Correct. For reasons I can't explain, your granddaughter decided it would be a good idea to try to sneak you into town when it wasn't safe," Circe said and Grandma scowled at me.

"Okay, okay, I get it. I screwed up bad. You don't have to rub it in," I groaned. "Grandma's here now and that's that. What are we going to do?"

"There's no better place for your grandmother to be than here," Circe said. "She can stay with me tonight, and possibly for a few more days if necessary until we can arrange for her to return home safely."

"And then what? Am I going to be put on trial?" I asked.

"As I said, you were lucky to be found by me and not someone else. Though I'm disappointed, I won't throw you under the broom, Zoe. Assuming we're able to fix this without anyone finding out — a rather brazen assumption — we can pretend it never happened and ensure it never happens again," Circe said.

"Thank you," I said. Though I had no right to her kindness after the way I'd gone behind her back, I was grateful for it regardless.

"Werewolves..." Grandma muttered, clearly off in her own world. Maybe that was just her way of coping with things.

"You need to get home. Does anyone else know about this? Anyone at all?" Circe asked.

"Just my roommate, Flora. Oh, and my cat, but I don't think that matters much," I said.

"Assuming she doesn't tell anyone what she knows, no, it shouldn't," Circe said.

"Luna wouldn't betray me," I said.

"Wait, Luna can talk?" Grandma asked.

"You've got a lot to learn, Gram," I sighed.

"But it won't be this time," Circe said. "Don't worry about her, Zoe. I'll make sure she's taken care of and has everything she needs until it's time to leave."

"Thank you again, I don't deserve this," I said, feeling intensely ashamed of myself. Circe and her sister Raina had bent over backward for me, and this was how I repaid them?

"I expect better of you going forward, Zoe," Circe said as she pointed her wand at me again. "Now go home and stay there. *Evanesco!*"

Seconds later, I found myself back in Flora's living room, my head buzzing. Flora screamed from where she sat on the couch and Luna jumped three feet in the air.

"Zoe! Are you okay? Where's your grandmother?" Flora asked as she rushed to me.

"She's at Circe's house. It's a long story," I sighed.

I'd screwed up everything.

CHAPTER FOUR

TRYING to stay focused at work the next day was like trying to walk on water. No matter what I looked at or what came across my desk, all I could think about was Grandma.

Though I knew she was safe at Circe's house, that didn't stop me worrying about the punishment I was sure to face for breaking the rules and defying the Council's ruling. That fear didn't get any better when I came across stories of things that had been destroyed by unruly werewolves overnight.

The fact that I hadn't run into any myself while I was out gallivanting in the dark was a miracle. Circe was right, it was lucky she found me and Grandma rather than someone else. I shuddered every time I thought about it.

"How are you holding up?" Flora asked and I jumped. I hadn't heard her come to my desk.

"Oh, you know, just another day," I laughed. The truth was I felt like I was coming unraveled.

"Aw, Zoe, I'm sorry. What do you think's going to happen?"

"I have no idea. Circe said she would keep it all under wraps for my sake, but that doesn't mean the word hasn't spread. If there's anything I've learned in my short time in this town it's that no one can keep a secret," I sighed.

Though the curfew was in place for everyone last night, I wondered if I was the only one out wandering around when I wasn't supposed to be. If it was as easy for me to get to the town gates as it was, was there anything stopping others from doing the same?

I just hoped no one saw me or Grandma. If word got out, it could be the end of me personally and professionally.

"Well, good luck. Try not to let your head get away from you in all this," Flora said.

"Easier said than done."

"Maybe you should go out and get some fresh air for a while. You know, to take your mind off things," Flora suggested.

It wasn't the worst idea in the world, and it wasn't the first time it'd occurred to me. If anything, I could use it as an excuse to drop by Town Hall to talk to Circe. Surely, if anyone had a comment to make about the Blood Moon and its effects, it would be one of the Councilmembers, right?

"Good idea. Will you tell Mitch I stepped out if he asks?"

"Sure thing," Flora said, smiling. "Don't worry, Zoe. Everything will be fine."

"I hope you're right," I said as I pushed back from my desk and headed outside.

Not even the sun's rays on my face made me feel much better. I was too worried I was about to be accosted by someone asking me questions, questions I couldn't answer.

Now I knew how it felt to be on the other side of an interview.

Though I'd seen reports about destroyed property, nothing in this part of town looked like it was out of sorts. Then again, maybe that wasn't much of a surprise. Who in their right mind would go after the Town Hall, even if they didn't have full control of themselves?

I shoved through the double doors to find the hall relatively empty. Maybe everyone was out doing cleanup control instead of sitting around debating policy. In any case, no one would notice if I slipped past, so I made my way down the hall toward Circe's office and knocked on the door.

No one answered. Was she even there? I could only imagine how busy Circe must've been after an eventful night like the one we'd just had, not to mention babysitting my grandmother.

I knocked again, louder this time, and the door flung open a few seconds later. Circe looked wild-eyed like she hadn't slept. That made two of us.

"Hey, can I talk to you for a few minutes?" I asked, gingerly. I had no right to even make the request, but there I was.

"About what?" Circe asked, eyeing me.

"About the Blood Moon. You know, for the Messenger," I lied, just in case anyone overheard.

"Come in and close the door behind you," Circe said, leaving me to stride back to her desk. I closed the door and stood rooted to the spot, unsure what to say.

"How is everything?" I asked when she didn't speak.

"Fine, all things considered," Circe said as she rummaged through the various stacks of papers on her desk. As cluttered as it was the last time I'd seen it, somehow it looked worse.

"What does that mean?"

"Your grandmother is understandably in a bit of shock after everything she's seen, but she's coping," Circe said and a stab of guilt wrenched in my stomach.

"I'm never going to be able to make this up to either one of you," I groaned.

"We shouldn't be talking about this here," Circe said.

"Why not? There's no one else around and it's not like they can hear through walls," I said.

Circe looked sideways at me. "Are you sure about that?" she asked.

"Fine. I guess I'd better get something for the paper while I'm here. Anything you care to share with me?"

"I'm sure you probably know more than I do at this point," Circe said.

"I heard there were several cases of damaged property. Do you know anything about that?" I asked.

"No, other than we're all lucky no one was injured," Circe said. "Particularly you."

"Circe, I'm so sorry, I—"

Circe held up a hand to silence me.

"As I said, not here," Circe said.

"Can I visit later?" I whispered. She nodded.

"So long as you aren't obvious and you're sure you won't be followed," Circe said.

"If I can sneak around town without getting caught under a curfew, I think I can manage to get to your house safely," I said. "But I guess you'll need to give me the address since I didn't exactly walk through the front door."

"Here, take a card," Circe said and reached for one of the business cards in a tray on her desk — probably the only thing in the entire room that was somewhat organized. She handed it over to me and I pocketed it without looking.

"After dark, no sooner," she whispered.

"Okay, I guess I'll see you then," I said.

"You can see yourself out, I've got things I need to take care of," Circe said. She was clearly upset with me, not that I blamed her, but I didn't know how to handle it. Nodding, I walked myself out of her office and back across the street to the Messenger, defeated.

It was going to be another long day waiting for sunset.

"SO SHE DIDN'T TELL you anything?" Flora asked, her arms crossed over her chest, her brows furrowed.

"Not really, no. Circe said Grandma was okay, but she wouldn't say anything more," I said.

"Well, I guess that's all we can really hope for, isn't it? I'm so sorry this happened, Zoe," she said.

"I'm just sorry I was dumb enough to think I could get away with it," I said.

"Clearly you're not the one with nine lives," Luna said from her spot between us on the couch.

We'd been sitting in the living room without saying much after work, all of us not-so-patiently waiting for the sun to set so I could visit Circe and Grandma.

"I guess not. I wonder what Grandma's been doing all day while Circe was at work," I said.

"I'm sure she's not having a hard time entertaining herself. She was never high maintenance," Luna said.

"I can't imagine how angry she must be with me," I sighed. "That's the worst part of all of this, knowing how much I let her down."

"Don't beat up on yourself too much," Flora said. "Though I obviously think you made a mistake, I think your heart was in the right place. I don't know that I would've been capable of making a better choice in your shoes."

"That's sweet of you to say, but you don't have to kiss up to me," I said. "Grandma will get over it eventually, I'm not too worried about her, but I don't know how I'm going to smooth things over with Circe or if it'll ever be the same again between us."

"Well, the only thing you can do is try. She likes you, maybe even loves you after the way you helped her solve her daughter's murder, so I don't think she'll hold it against you for too long," Flora said.

"I hope not," I said, staring out the window as the sun sank below the trees.

"Do you know where you're going?" Flora asked. I pulled out the card Circe had given me and held it up so Flora could read it.

"Not exactly, but I'm sure I can figure it out. It looks that she doesn't live far from her sister over on Moonbeam," I said.

"Good. It won't look suspicious if anyone sees you walking through the Witches' Quarter," Flora said.

"Well, I guess I should get this over with," I sighed as I stood from the couch.

"It'll be fine. Maybe Circe already has a ticket booked to send your grandmother home and she's just waiting for you to come over to say goodbye," Flora said.

"That would be the best case scenario, but somehow I doubt it," I said.

"Good luck," Flora said as I stepped out the front door and walked idly toward the Witches' Quarter in the northwest part of town. The moon had mostly returned to normal, though a red tinge lingered and it was still a little larger than it should've been.

I turned left on Moonbeam Avenue and walked past number three, Raina's house, hoping Circe hadn't yet shared everything with her sister. It was bad enough I'd disappointed Circe; I couldn't handle disappointing both of the Woods sisters.

As I approached the end of the street and number twelve, the address listed on the business card Circe gave me, I noticed a faint green light flickering above the trees that surrounded her house.

I picked up my pace, panic gripping my chest, and let out a gasp when I rounded the corner to find Circe's house ablaze in bright green flames that could only have been magical.

"No!" I screamed as I pulled my wand from my robes and ran toward the house, but skidded to a halt when the flames surged. The front door was wide open, but there wasn't any indication Circe and Grandma had escaped.

Everywhere I looked there was fire, a kind I'd never seen in my life. I racked my brain trying to think of a spell, anything that might help me put out the fire, but nothing came. As if my wand could read my desperation, sparks began to fly from its tip.

"Zoe!" a voice sputtered and I squinted to find Grandma on her hands and knees among the bushes on the side of the house, her clothes covered in soot. I raced over to her and my ankle rolled as I stepped on something hard and round, sending me tumbling to the ground. What the…?

I flailed in the dirt to find a golden piece that looked like some sort of stopper for a vial. Annoyed, I picked it up and tucked it into my robes to keep anyone else from tripping on it. I crawled to Grandma and examined her for any signs of injury. Aside from some burns on her clothes, she seemed to be fine.

"What happened?"

"I don't know," Grandma croaked, her voice raw from smoke

inhalation. She coughed, the wheezing seizing her entire body, and I threw my arms around her. Thank Lilith she was okay — but where was Circe?

"Did you see anything? Was it something inside the house that caught fire?" I asked, frantic.

"No clue. I was in the living room and Circe was in the kitchen makin' us some tea. Next thing I know, the house explodes in green and I can't see or breathe or nothin' so I did what they told us to do as kids: I got on my hands and knees and crawled out the front door," Grandma said.

"I'm so glad you're okay," I said and hugged her again, ignoring the sharp stench of smoke on her clothes. Was Circe still in the house, and if she was, how could I get her out without getting hurt myself?

"Ain't no way you can go in there, Zoe," Grandma said. She must've read it on my face.

"I have to do something, I can't just leave her in there," I said.

"You're a witch now, ain't you? Can't you put out the fire with some spell or other?"

"I just got this thing, I barely know how to hold it, much less use it," I said, slapping my wand against my leg as it continued to spark. Was it broken? Or was it just me who was broken?

"There's gotta be somethin'. Think fast, Sugar!" Grandma said. I released her and stood up, recalling every one of the few magical lessons I'd had since getting the wand. Nothing came to mind to help put out a fire, but maybe that wasn't what I needed now.

I held my wand straight up into the air and closed my eyes, willing the magic coursing through my blood to flow into the wand. It vibrated in my hand and when I opened my eyes, sparks shot from its tip into the sky and exploded like fireworks.

If no one knew about the fire yet, they definitely would now.

"'Atta girl!" Grandma shouted before another coughing fit took over her.

I helped Grandma up off the ground and walked her as far away as possible just to be safe. With flames that high and unpredictable, there was no telling if or when the roof might collapse.

Every second counted, so I breathed a sigh of relief when I heard police sirens roar to life in the distance, barely audible over the roar of the flames. The cops might not be able to put out the fire, but they could probably save Circe if she was in danger.

"Zoe, look!" Grandma shouted, pointing up. A group of eight warlocks in bright red robes and matching caps darted overhead on broomsticks in a V-formation with their wands drawn. Apparently, Moon Grove had a magical fire department I didn't know about.

The firefighters cast spell after spell, water jetting from their wand tips in torrents, but no matter how much water they threw at the flames, they didn't extinguish — and every time water made contact with the blaze, it spattered and spread like grease, igniting the nearest trees.

"Guys! There's someone inside!" I shouted up at them.

The lead firefighter in the V-shape who seemed to be heading the effort thudded to the ground next to me. He was broad-shouldered, muscular, and towered over me like a human skyscraper.

"I'm Fire Chief Blaine Hart. Who's inside?" he asked.

"Councilwoman Woods," I answered.

Blaine's piercing blue eyes widened, but he nodded and cast some sort of protective spell over himself.

"Stay put, both of you," he said and ran undeterred through the front door into the heart of the fire. Amazingly, though the flames licked at him and his robes, they did no damage. I watched until the green inferno inside the house swallowed him.

"Is he out of his cotton-pickin' mind?!" Grandma shouted.

"He's a professional, he knows what he's doing," I said — at least I hoped.

The other firefighters seemed to have realized their approach was only making things worse. They transitioned to launching sand from their wands to try to suffocate the fire, but not even that worked.

Minutes that felt like hours passed as I waited for any sign of Blaine. Grandma took my hand in hers and squeezed it so hard I thought it might lose all circulation.

"I hope like heck she's okay," Grandma muttered.

"Me too, Gram," I said.

The blame for this fell squarely on my shoulders. Had someone seen or heard about Grandma Elle staying at Circe's? Had they firebombed her house to hurt me or Circe or both?

If I hadn't tried to sneak Grandma into town, none of this would've happened.

"Zoe!" Grandma said, yanking my hand to jolt me back into reality. She pointed straight ahead and I squinted to make out Blaine's silhouette as he powered through the flames that consumed the house. Circe's body bounced lifelessly in his arms as he walked, her robes blackened.

The crackling of the roof collapsing and the whoosh of the air shooting out was all I heard as my whole world spun away from me in a haze of green embers and the acrid smell of smoke.

Circe was dead.

CHAPTER FIVE

FOR THE SECOND time in as many days, the Council of Moon Grove stared down at me from their high-backed chairs — one more of which was now empty.

My heart sank at the sight. I kept my eyes locked on my hands clasped tightly in front of me so no one could see them shaking. I wouldn't have any defenders here today.

The Town Hall was packed with people eager to see me get knocked down a peg or two. After all the people I'd brought to justice, maybe it was right of them to think that way.

Still, before I'd even gotten the summons to appear before the Council that morning I knew it was going to be a media spectacle. I could already see the sensationalized headlines splashed across the front page of Grave Times: Moon Grove's Golden Girl Tarnished; Star Reporter Falls From Heavens; Councilwoman Dies in Fire, Torching Reporter's Reputation.

No matter how I sliced it, it wasn't going to be pretty.

At least the Council allowed me company this time. My friends and family lined the table: Beau immediately to my left, Grandma on my right, and Flora beside her. Beau reached under the table to pat my leg and I nearly jumped out of my skin.

"It's going to be okay, one way or the other," Beau whispered in my ear. It wasn't nearly as comforting as I'm sure he wanted it to be. I didn't know what to say so I nodded and rested my head against his.

"We're here for you, Sugar," Grandma said. "I won't let 'em give you the runaround."

Of all people, I didn't deserve Elle's support. I'd lied to her and brought her to Moon Grove under false pretenses and almost gotten her killed in a house fire. Some granddaughter, right?

Heath cleared his throat and slammed his gavel against its stand three times to bring everyone to attention.

I worried I might pass out. Public speaking — much less public humiliation — was never really my thing. For Lilith's sake, I'd run screaming from my elementary school's talent show when Elle volunteered me for it, so the thought of standing in front of all of Moon Grove and confessing my sins was breathtaking.

"My fellow citizens of Moon Grove, it's with a heavy heart that I've gathered us all here today," Heath said, his voice low and somber. Bags hung under his eyes and I wondered if he'd gotten as little sleep — or less — as the rest of us.

"As I'm sure you are all well aware by now, last night we lost a dear friend and fellow Councilmember, Circe Woods."

The hall was so quiet I heard my heart hammering in my chest. What could anyone say?

"Life in Moon Grove has been tumultuous in the last few weeks, and Councilwoman Woods' passing is only the most recent in a wave of unfortunate events."

Unfortunate events? That was one heck of a way of dressing it up.

"I wanted to be transparent with you all. However, because the case is still under investigation and the facts are murky, we won't be sharing any further details today," Heath continued.

"As such, at this time we'd like to request everyone but Zoe and her grandmother leave the room," Heath said, and I sat bolt upright in my chair. Why would they bother letting me bring all my family and friends only to send them out again when I needed them most?

Evidently, everyone else agreed because grumblings carried throughout the room. Heath slammed his gavel down again until it was silent.

"Rest assured, you will be kept abreast of any developments. I have no doubt our upstanding publications will make sure you know everything you need to know in due time," he said. "Now please, show yourselves out in an orderly fashion so we can proceed."

"Don't panic. At least you'll still have your grandmother," Beau said as he let go of my hand and kissed the top of my head. "I'll be right outside waiting for you when it's over."

"Thank you," I said, hearing my voice as if I were outside myself. With a nod and a somber smile, Beau stood and left the room along with Flora. They each waved at me one last time as if to wish me luck, but it didn't help. Grandma scooted her chair closer to mine.

"Don't you worry your purty little head, Granny's right here," Grandma whispered.

Minutes later, the hall was completely empty save for me, Grandma, and the eleven remaining Council members. None of them looked me in the eye. Maybe they were afraid they'd burst into flame too if they did.

"Zoe, it goes without saying how troubled we are about all this," Heath said. I didn't have a response so I stared straight ahead.

"Would you like to start by telling us your account?"

I nodded and swallowed hard, hoping I didn't break down in the middle of my description. Grandma squeezed my hand to encourage me.

"It's a long story, but I guess I'll start from the beginning," I said, my voice cracking.

I told them about everything: how I'd gone behind their backs and lied to Grandma to get her to come to Moon Grove because I felt like the Council owed me a return favor; how I'd snuck out during the curfew to meet Grandma at the town gates; and how Circe caught us and warped us back to her house.

"Let me be clear: your grandmother was staying with Councilwoman Woods by the Councilwoman's own suggestion?" Heath asked.

"Yessir. Zoe's got the right of it. Circe cast a spell to send us back to her house and told me I could stay there until she figured out how to get me back to my farm," Grandma said.

Heath seemed surprised to hear from Grandma at all, especially since she'd answered a question for me. "I ain't tryin' to be rude," she continued, "but Zoe's havin' a hard time with all this."

"Understandably so," Heath said. "But Zoe, none of us thinks you're responsible for the death of Councilwoman Woods. We all know you better than that."

"Thank you," I said, my throat tightening as tears threatened to overtake me again, though the look on Lorelei Riddle's face said otherwise.

I hadn't felt this shaken or discouraged since I got fired from my job before coming to Moon Grove. Being in the magical town and learning everything it had to offer, about my family's history and my place in the world of magic, gave me a new sense of confidence — but at that moment under the Council's microscope, I felt smaller than a werewolf's hair.

"That said, it would be irresponsible of us not to point out how reckless your actions were," Heath said. He didn't need to remind me, nor did he need to beat me up for it — I'd done more than enough of that myself over the last twelve hours.

"But I don't want to belabor the point. As it stands now, we're simply trying to understand what happened. Please, tell us what you saw, anything at all, that might be of use to the investigation," he said.

"I didn't see much, or at least nothing out of the ordinary. I went to visit Councilwoman Woods in her office yesterday afternoon to check in with her and see how my grandmother was doing, but she refused to talk about it in these walls," I said.

"Which was probably a smart idea, given the circumstances and the preponderance of new journalists lurking around," Heath said.

"Right. So Circe invited me over after dark when it was less likely anyone would see or potentially follow me," I said.

"Of course. So, you did make it to Councilwoman Woods' house?"

"After the fire had already started, yes," I said. I closed my eyes and all I could see was the bright green flames as if they were coming right at me all over again, threatening to devour me.

"I see. So you didn't see anyone or anything suspicious when you arrived?"

"Other than the green flames spewing from the roof, no," I said, though it brought to mind the golden stopper I'd tripped on.

It was still in the pocket of my robes, but I'd forgotten all about it thanks to the whirl of everything else going on. After Fire Chief Hart handed Circe's body over to the police, Police Chief Mueller whisked me away to the station to get our official statements since Grandma and I were the only known witnesses.

"And what about you, Mrs. Clarke?" Heath asked Grandma, and she perked up like she'd been electrocuted. "What did you see? You were inside the building when the fire started, were you not?"

"Yessir," Grandma said. I'd never seen her so uncomfortable in her own skin before, but then again, I'd also never seen her on trial — not that this was an official trial yet, but it might as well have been.

"And can you tell us what you remember of that night?"

"It was simple, all things bein' considered," Grandma started. "I mean, aside from me learning about all y'all magic folks and werewolves and whatnot, it wasn't nothin' out of the ordinary. Councilman Woods and I were chattin' about my arrival and about Zoe and then she offered to make us some tea."

"Sounds normal enough," he said.

"I reckon it was until the whole darn place blew up," Grandma said.

"Spontaneously? No warning whatsoever?" Heath asked.

"No, none. I was sittin' in the living room while Circe made tea in the kitchen behind me. All sort of things were runnin' through my head about what I'd seen and been through, so I wasn't really payin' much attention, I reckon, until everything turned all green and smoky," Grandma said.

"So you're saying you had nothing to do with the fire?" Lorelei interrupted and my blood turned cold. How dare she suggest my grandmother had anything to do with this?

"I beg your pardon?" Grandma asked, clearly as offended as I was.

"You were the only other person in the house with Councilwoman Woods at the time of the fire. It's a reasonable question," Lorelei said. She refused to look at me, which probably wasn't a bad thing because I wouldn't have been able to hold my tongue if she had.

Was she doing this to get back at me for putting her daughter, Aurelia, in jail? It wouldn't have surprised me.

"Councilwoman Riddle has a point," another witch on the Council said, the first time I'd heard her speak. She was a small woman who hunched forward, and glasses that were two times bigger than her face rested on her large, hooked nose.

"As uncomfortable as the question may be, it must be asked," the witch said, her voice wavering. She must've been one of the eldest members on the Council.

"Thank you, Councilwoman Bloodworth," Lorelei said, and I could've sworn I saw a smile flash across her face. The suggestion was absurd. Grandma Elle didn't believe in killing spiders who wandered into her house, much less a witch who'd shown her hospitality.

"Forgive us, Zoe, but you must understand things from our perspective. You violated Moon Grove's rules and went against our decision to bring a family member into our town, and on the very night you did so, one of our colleagues died in a house fire. The optics aren't good," Heath said.

I sat stewing, unable to speak. The message was loud and clear: I messed up big time. But that didn't mean they had to throw my grandmother under the broom.

"I ain't trying to say you ain't right to be worried or to ask the question, but what reason could a little ol' lady like me possibly have to light the darn house on fire with me still in it?" Grandma asked. At least someone in the room had their senses about them.

"That's a good question, and an answer we're still trying to find," Heath said. "Unfortunately, answers are exceedingly hard to come by so we must turn over every stone."

"Enough!" a voice boomed through the hall, making all of us jump. I whirled in my seat to find a witch who looked the spitting image of Circe striding down the hall toward the Council, her royal purple robes flowing behind her like a cape.

It was Raina Woods, Circe's sister and Headmistress of Moon Grove's Veilside Academy of Magic.

Her mouth was a thin line and her auburn hair was pulled back in as severe of a bun as I'd ever seen her wear. As she passed my chair, she purposely ignored me. Of all people to make a surprise entrance to defend me, Raina was the last one I would've guessed.

"Headmistress, it's good of you to join us, though I must say I'm surprised given the grief you must be experiencing," Heath said.

Lorelei's face soured at the sight of Raina like she'd gotten something foul stuck under her nose, a detail I didn't miss. It wasn't any secret that there was bad blood between the Woods and Riddle families, but this was something else entirely.

"There's plenty of time for grieving, but there's no time for a mockery like this," Raina said.

Heath coughed. "Headmistress, I mean no disrespect, but it isn't up to you to decide what's a waste of the Council's time, no matter your relation to its members."

"No, of course it isn't, but it becomes my business when one of my star students is dragged through the mud and made a fool of in public simply because she made a mistake, which I'm sure I need not remind you is rare for Ms. Clarke," Raina said.

Seconds passed as Raina and Heath stared each other down, neither of them budging, and I worried for a moment the intense energy between them might light the Town Hall on fire too.

"If there's something you've come to say in defense of Ms. Clarke, by all means, the floor is yours," Heath said at last.

"It's clear that Ms. Clarke made a grave mistake, perhaps even a series of them, last evening," Raina said, addressing the entire Council as she paced back and forth in front of them — still without meeting my eyes.

"An understatement if I've ever heard one," Lorelei said just loudly enough for everyone to hear and Raina snapped around to fix her with her intense gaze. "Ms. Clarke is lucky we're even entertaining hearing what she has to say. As far as I'm concerned, she put the entirety of Moon Grove at risk last night and she should be expelled as a result."

My heart dropped into my stomach. Could they really do that? Would they really do that to me, after one less-than-stellar night in my track record?

I felt like I was going to be sick.

"And as far as I'm concerned, it sounds to me like the lot of you are inciting a witch hunt," Raina said. "You have no evidence, nothing at all to stand on, other than your own personal feelings, good or bad, towards Ms. Clarke. That's hardly fair."

If Raina ever needed a second job, she should really consider becoming a lawyer — assuming witches and warlocks had a use for those.

"Should we just let her walk away with a slap on the wrist to put us in danger again in the future then?" Lorelei challenged, leaning forward in her chair.

"No, of course not. Look at Ms. Clarke. Is it not abundantly clear that she realizes the gravity of her mistakes? Don't you think she regrets everything she's done and would take it back in a heartbeat if she could?" Raina asked.

"Her regret won't bring your sister back," Lorelei said, and Raina looked like she'd been slapped across the face.

"Nor will your desperate charge to convict her of something for which you have no proof," Raina said. "I've had the pleasure of getting to know Zoe better than any of you, and I know in my heart she's not capable of something as heinous as this. It's absurd to suggest otherwise."

"I think we've heard enough!" Heath shouted as Lorelei opened her mouth to retort. "Thank you for your perspective, Headmistress."

"To be clear, I'm not recommending Zoe receive no punishment. My only request is that any discipline is measured and matched to what we know for a fact she's done wrong," Raina said.

It stung to hear, but she was right to say it.

"Then what *do* you recommend?" Heath asked.

Finally, Raina turned to look at me. Though she tried to maintain her stern, disapproving look, I saw under the surface how much it hurt.

As awful as Grandma's disappointment felt, disappointing Raina was infinitely worse. Had it not been for her, I never would've learned anything about magic or my family's links to magical history, or been invited to Veilside — and now her sister was dead.

Raina mouthed "I'm sorry" to me and turned back to the Council.

"Confiscate her wand. Until she can prove she's trustworthy again, she won't need it. Additionally, her studies at Veilside will be suspended until further notice," Raina said and I thought I might pass out.

Lorelei smirked down at me. I hadn't had my wand long at all, but now that it was being taken away from me, I felt like I'd taken eight steps backward in terms of my magical advancement. It was devastating.

Lesson learned.

"And what about her grandmother?" Heath asked.

"She can stay with me," Raina said. "That way I can keep an eye on things."

I didn't like that idea, but it served two purposes because we didn't have room for Grandma at Flora's house — and it wasn't like I could argue in my position.

"That sounds reasonable. I think we should put it to a vote, however, for the sake of the official record. All those in favor of Headmistress Woods' proposals, raise your wands and say 'aye,'" Heath said.

Every single witch and warlock on the Council — including Grace Magnus — raised their wands. The decision was unanimous. It wasn't surprising, but it still hurt.

"So it shall be done," Heath said and waved his wand at me. Mine wiggled out of its place in my robes and soared into his free hand. I felt defenseless without it, even though I didn't really know how to use any real magic yet.

And now I might never get the chance to learn. The only way I could prove myself to the Council and the rest of Moon Grove was to figure out who really killed Circe and why.

I reached into my robes to palm the golden vial stopper I'd found at the scene of the crime. I had no idea what it really was or how it had ended up at Circe's house, and I had no proof, but I couldn't shake the feeling it was central to everything.

Whatever it took, I would find out for Grandma's sake and my own.

"Let this be a lesson, Ms. Clarke, that no one is above the Council — not even you," Heath said. "Do you have anything you'd like to say?"

I pushed back from the table and stood, my entire body trembling.

"I'll make this right. I promise I will," I said, my voice shaking.

"Thank you, Zoe," Heath said. "You may go."

I left with Grandma and Raina at my heels. Beau threw his arms around me when we stepped outside, which I was grateful for because I refused to let Lorelei or anyone else on the Council see me cry.

CHAPTER SIX

I STRODE into the Messenger's offices the next morning on a mission, ignoring all the stares from my colleagues — most of whom I still hadn't formally met.

There wasn't a doubt in my mind that they all had opinions about me and my actions but I didn't have the time or space in my brain to care. The only thing that mattered was figuring out who killed Circe, how they did it, and why.

"Zoe," Mitch barked from the other side of the office where he stood waiting with his arms across his chest, scowling.

Evidently, he had other plans.

Sighing, I tossed my bag down on my desk and made my way over to Mitch. I couldn't avoid him all day, so better to get whatever he wanted to say to me out of the way now.

He ushered me into his office and closed the door softly behind us. Maybe he wasn't angry after all.

"I'm sure you know why I called you in here," Mitch said. He sank down into his chair, which groaned and protested under his weight.

The armrests, which were already shredded to ribbons the first time I saw them, looked like they'd only gotten worse in the last few days — no doubt thanks to the Blood Moon's effects on Mitch as a werewolf.

"Yeah, I can guess," I said.

"Look, I'm not here to beat up on you. I'm sure you've already gotten plenty of that from everyone else," Mitch said. "The only thing I'm concerned about is how this is going to reflect on the Messenger and our work, specifically yours."

"I can't possibly answer that," I said.

"No, I didn't think you could. But I think we need to come up with some sort of plan because something tells me that this isn't going to be the last we hear of this," Mitch said.

"I think the best thing we can do is to keep doing what we've always done: get to the truth. That's exactly what I intend to do, anyway," I said.

A wide smile split Mitch's face, a rarity for him. He stroked his beard and nodded.

"Good, I like your attitude. I take it that means you're going to try to figure out who's responsible for all this?" Mitch asked.

"Sure am," I said.

"Any ideas? Any leads?" Mitch asked.

I hemmed and hawed for a second, debating whether or not I wanted to tell him about the vial stopper I'd found. To most people, it was a tiny detail that didn't mean anything, but I couldn't let it go.

"Promise not to laugh if I tell you?" I asked.

"Well, I won't promise, but I'll try not to," Mitch said, smirking. Any other time his sarcasm would've gotten on my nerves, but after everything I'd been through lately, I appreciated the lighthearted approach.

"Fine, here goes," I said and reached into my robes to pull out the stopper.

It was small, not quite big enough to fill my palm as I held it out in front of him. Mitch squinted to get a better look at it and looked back up at me with his eyebrows furrowed.

"What's that?" he asked.

"A Golden Snitch, duh," I said and Mitch only looked more confused. I'd forgotten no one here was going to get my clichéd Harry Potter references.

"I'm not sure what it is honestly. If I had to guess, I'd say it's some sort of stopper for a vial or a chemical beaker or something," I said.

"Where did you find it?"

"Well, it found me actually. I tripped on this thing trying to get to my grandma during the house fire," I said as I rolled the stopper around in my palm. The light caught it a certain way and for the first time, I noticed there was something engraved in its surface.

"Wait a second, there's some sort of symbol on here," I said, holding it closer to my face to get a better look. A faintly-etched diamond with an open eye inside stared back at me.

"What is it?"

"I don't know, I don't recognize it," I said and pinched it between two fingers to allow Mitch to see.

"I don't recognize it either but it looks like it's some sort of philosophical thing," Mitch said.

"This has to be connected somehow."

"Okay, maybe it is, but how?"

"That's what I'm trying to figure out. Why was it outside Circe's front door? I'm telling you, Mitch, that fire wasn't normal. The flames were bright green and no matter what the firefighters did, the flames wouldn't extinguish, they just spread," I said.

The firefighters eventually had to give up and let the flames die out themselves when they got down to the dirt and had nothing left to use as fuel.

"Okay, so you think they were magical or something?"

"They must've been. I don't know if it was fire cast by a spell or if it was some sort of potion, but given that I found this stopper nearby, I'm willing to bet it had something to do with alchemy," I said.

"Interesting. You're right, it's not much, but I guess it's as good a place to start as any," he said.

"It's all I've got, so it'll have to be," I said.

"Wait a second, what about that new tonic shop that just opened up? What's it called again?" Mitch asked and immediately the crazed and dazed face of Hilda Blackwood appeared in my mind. My heart jumped up into my throat.

"Hypnotic Tonics, of course, why didn't I think of that?!" I shouted. The answer, obviously, was that I had a lot of other things on my mind so spotting clues wasn't as easy as it usually was for me.

"Yeah, that's the one. The owner of the place was at the announcement of the curfew. She was the one who made the prediction about death, wasn't she? I don't know about you, but that seems a little too coincidental to me," Mitch said.

"I doubt someone who was planning to murder would announce it to the entire town like that, but who knows, stranger things have happened here," I said with a shrug.

"Maybe you should go talk to her to see what she tells you — and what she doesn't. She might have some sort of tonic to block you from reading her thoughts, but the only way to find out is to try," Mitch said.

"That's a great idea," I said. "The only problem is I'm going to need some sort of alibi. Everyone in town knows I'm tied to what happened to Circe, so I doubt they'll be willing to talk to me if I don't give them a believable reason."

"True. Well, Hypnotic Tonics is a new shop in town. Maybe you could use the excuse that you're writing a story about the shop itself or a boom in small business for Moon Grove?" Mitch suggested.

"Oh, I love that. The owner's probably desperate for positive coverage after her little premonition came true," I said. "But wait, are we really going to run a story like that?"

"I guess it depends on what you get out of her," Mitch said, smiling.

"Challenge accepted," I said and pocketed the stopper. "Do you know where her shop is?"

"Yeah, it's at the corner of Crescent and Cartier just a couple of blocks from here," Mitch said. "It's a little, well, eccentric, to say the least. Trust me, you can't miss it."

"Good. Something tells me Ms. Blackwood and I have a lot to talk about," I said and turned to open the door.

"Hey Zoe," Mitch called, freezing me in my tracks. "Don't let this Circe situation or anything else take that spark away from you. It's what makes you who you are and what made me hire you in the first place."

It almost made me cry. Mitch was right — now of all times, I couldn't afford to doubt myself. I might've made a major mistake and paid a grave cost for it, but I couldn't ignore the fact that it all could've just as easily been a coincidence.

It occurred to me as well that this might have been a setup. But who would want to frame me and my family for something like this? There was a long list of people I'd made enemies out of in my time in Moon Grove, but would any of them really want to hurt me like this?

I had to find out, one way or another.

"Thank you, Mitch," I said. "I know we don't always see eye to eye on things, but I'm really glad to have you as my boss."

"You've probably shaved off at least ten years of my life since you started working here, but I wouldn't have it any other way," Mitch said, beaming. "Now enough with the sappy stuff, get out there and get the truth."

With a nod, I stepped out of Mitch's office and went back to my desk. If anyone could help me figure out what the symbol on the stopper was, it would be Mallory Crane, my one and only friend from Veilside — and the best researcher in Moon Grove.

I snatched my phone out of my bag. Thankfully, it'd come back to life after I re-entered town with Grandma. I held the stopper out in front of me and snapped a picture of the engraving before I sent it to Mallory with a short message:

>> Me: *Hey, sorry for the radio silence. Had a lot going on. Anyway, does this image ring any bells for you? Asking for a friend.*

Unsurprisingly, Mallory answered instantaneously.

>> Mallory: *That's okay, I knew from all the news reports you were alive, though I'm sure you wish you weren't right about now. I think I've seen that symbol somewhere before but I can't remember where. I'll see what I can find.*

>> Me: *Thanks. Let's get lunch or something soon to catch up, I feel like I haven't seen you in forever.*

>> Mallory: *Yeah, that's what happens when you get suspended from school, you sling blade renegade.*

>> Me: *Very funny. I gotta go, talk to you soon.*

>> Mallory: *Okay, try not to break any more rules between now and then.*

Rolling my eyes, I threw my phone back in my bag and headed outside. At least the weather was nice. The sun was already high in the sky, shining merrily like it was smiling, and it was difficult for me not to smile back at it. As awful as things had gotten, I was back on track doing what I did best: asking questions.

IT TOOK LESS than three minutes for me to walk the distance from the Messenger to Hypnotic Tonics and only about three seconds to realize how right Mitch was about the place.

The building was tiny, roughly the size of a studio apartment. Neon, mismatched garden decorations in the shape of various flora — most of them mushrooms — lined the walkway leading to the front door, which itself was painted tie-dye.

A humming case that appeared to be a vending machine sat to the right of the door, displaying rows of brightly-colored potions in bulbous glass vials for any passersby to purchase. None of the concoctions were labeled, but suddenly it was no wonder Hilda seemed to be on something during the Council meeting — based on what I'd seen of her shop, she probably was.

I walked up the pathway, pushed the front door open, and bells and chimes greeted me as I stepped inside. Hilda sat on a plush violet cushion in the center of the room, her eyes closed, seemingly deep in meditation. Not even the sound of me entering had disturbed her.

Unsure of what else to do, I waited for Hilda to notice me, but nothing happened. I cleared my throat to try to get her attention, but all it did was scare a snore out of her. Things were already off to a great start.

"Hilda?" I asked carefully. I didn't want to scare her out of her skin, but I couldn't just stand there waiting forever. She grunted and her wild eyes fluttered open behind her Coke-bottle glasses; her world swam into focus and Hilda jolted when she realized I was standing there.

"Yes, good afternoon, dear," she said, jumping up off the cushion like someone half her age. "I'm sorry to keep you waiting, I was deep in contemplation."

Contemplation? Is that what the kids were calling it these days?

"That's okay, I'm not in any hurry," I said. As long as she told me what I needed to know, I would wait all day.

"Wait a moment, I recognize you," Hilda said, looking me up and down. She squinted her eyes to get a better look at me.

"You're Zoe Clarke," she said.

"Yup, that's me," I said. At some point, the novelty of me being me would have to wear off for everybody, but evidently, that wasn't today.

"Welcome, dear, though I must say it's a surprise. Have you come for a specific tonic? Perhaps something to ease anxiety?" Hilda asked, and I wasn't sure if she was being helpful or catty.

For half a second, I considered taking her up on the offer — but I had to keep my head clear, which didn't seem to be the focus of any of her tonics.

"No, actually, I came to talk to you about your shop. I'm writing an article for the Messenger about it and small business generally in Moon Grove. Do you have a few minutes to talk?" I asked.

Hilda eyed me like she didn't believe a word I'd said.

"You're not going to print anything salacious, are you?" she asked as she pushed her glasses up her nose.

"No, of course not," I lied. That depended on what she had to say. "I just figured you could use a bit of positive press after that unsettling Council meeting. Why would you think otherwise?"

"Because the Council's got it out for us," a voice said from behind me and I turned on my heel to find a young, sandy-haired witch standing behind a glass display case with her hands in the pockets of her tie-dyed robes. She looked just as unusual as Hilda, if not more.

"Don't say that, Sage," Hilda hissed. "Zoe, this is my apprentice, Sage Snow. Please don't write anything she says in your article. Though she's as smart as an elf, she enjoys exaggeration."

"Uh, okay, but why would she say it if it wasn't true?"

"Because it is true," Sage said, stepping around the display toward me. Her face was freckled and a thick gold ring hanging from her septum swayed back and forth with her movement.

"That doesn't make any sense. Why would the Council have it out for you?" I asked her.

"Some of them really don't like what we do here," Sage said. "They think our tonics are dangerous."

"Are they?" I asked as memories of the roaring green flames that consumed Circe's house came to mind.

"No, of course, they aren't!" Hilda said, her voice shrill. "We've passed all the safety checks and meet or exceed all Moon Grove regulations for consumable goods."

"Consumable goods?"

"Yes, dear, what did you think you were supposed to do with a tonic? Sniff it?" Hilda asked and Sage chuckled.

"So I take it these tonics induce some sort of magical effects on whoever drinks them?"

"You catch on quick," Sage said under her breath, but I let it go. I was trying to lead Hilda down a particular path and though my questions had obvious answers, I needed her to confirm what I already suspected.

"Precisely," Hilda said, ignoring Sage too.

"Do you have a best seller? Anything in particular that people come looking for?" I asked as I stepped around Sage to eye the rainbow of different potions inside the cases that lined each of the shop's walls — and froze when I realized a diamond with an open eye stared back at me from the golden stopper of each vial.

"Oh, most people love the Mean Green," Sage said and Hilda hissed her quiet, but I barely absorbed the words.

I couldn't stop staring at the symbol on the vials. There was no mistaking it; it was the same one on the stopper I'd found by Circe's house. But did that mean Hilda was involved directly or did it just mean that whoever lit Circe's house on fire was a fan of Hypnotic Tonics?

But wait a second, Mean Green? The name couldn't have been a coincidence. As interesting as it was, I had to keep a level head because if I asked too much too soon, Hilda would shut down. Sage, however...

"Why's it called the Mean Green?" I asked Sage.

"Because it's a green color, obviously, and it sends people's energy levels into overdr—"

"An elevated state so that they can safely get more done in less time," Hilda interrupted, speaking so quickly I barely understood her. She glared at Sage and deep red patches appeared on Sage's cheeks.

"Right, what she said," Sage said, staring down at the floor.

"Okay, so the green part makes sense, but I'm still not understanding why you'd call your best selling product 'mean,'" I said.

Hilda shuffled her feet. "Some of our products have unintended side effects," she admitted, avoiding my gaze.

"Yikes, like what? Fever? Dry skin? Bad breath? Stomachache? I mean, how bad are we talking here?"

"The Mean Green can produce hallucinogenic effects in a small subset of users," Hilda said and my eyes went wide. Having boosted energy while seeing things that weren't there seemed like a recipe for disaster to me — especially when a Blood Moon was mixed in for good measure.

Suddenly, the "Mean" part made perfect sense. But which kind of users was Hilda talking about?

"When I first approached the Council with my business proposal, that was their biggest concern. Some of the Councilmembers, in particular, felt that allowing the shop to open would lead to further, well, unintended consequences among the population," Hilda said.

Right, like lighting one of the Councilmembers' houses on fire while in a psychedelic fog.

"I bet I can guess who had hangups about it," I said.

"It doesn't matter who did. All that matters now is that we were allowed to open and that we're doing everything we can to be responsible business people in the community," Hilda said.

How many times had she rehearsed that answer?

"Right, obviously. That said, I'm sure you've heard by now about what happened to one of the members of the Council," I said, dancing around the subject. Hilda's shoulders rocketed up to her ears and I could practically see her rear end puckering.

"Yes, of course. Absolutely dreadful, that whole situation," Hilda said, her face nearly as red as Sage's.

"Some are saying it's not exactly a coincidence that one of the Councilmembers died shortly after your shop opened," I said.

Hilda stared me in the eye, the blush on her face deepening to a rage-filled purple.

"Ms. Clarke, I do hope you're not suggesting that I or my products had something to do with Councilwoman Woods' murder," she said. "More than that, if I remember correctly, you came to write a piece about our shop, not this."

"Sorry, I didn't mean any offense. It's just something I've heard talking to people around town," I lied as I thumbed the vial stopper in the pocket of my robes. Whether or not Hilda knew it, and whether or not she wanted to admit it, Hypnotic Tonics was linked to the murder somehow.

"Well, you know what they say about rumors, Ms. Clarke; they do spread like wildfire, don't they?" Hilda asked and a chill ran down my spine. Did she mean…?

"In any case, it wasn't Councilwoman Woods who gave us trouble, so why would we want to hurt her even if we were the type to be vindictive?" Hilda asked.

That changed things.

"If not Circe, who?"

"Lorelei Riddle," Sage spat. Hilda scowled at her like she'd uttered one of the worst words in the English language.

"As I said, Sage is prone to exaggeration," Hilda said. "While it's true we were subject to more scrutiny from Councilwoman Riddle than the others, it was nothing out of the ordinary."

"Did she have issues with your shop or with you personally?" I asked.

Lorelei seemed like she'd be the type to judge someone for their looks and hobbies — her daughter was the same way — and I was willing to bet Lorelei wasn't above using her powers for less-than-honorable means. After my run-ins with the Council lately, I knew firsthand.

"Both," Hilda said. "She seemed to connect the two in her mind as something detrimental to the community overall."

Sage scoffed.

"What she's really saying is that Lorelei accused us of being dirty hippies who were just trying to get all of Moon Grove hooked on tonics in a get-rich-quick scheme," Sage said, clearly not caring about Hilda's scorn anymore.

Yup, that sounded like something Lorelei would say.

"It doesn't seem that way to me. As far as I can tell, you guys are just trying to make it like the rest of us," I said with a shrug.

"Thank you. If only everyone else saw things that way," Hilda sighed. "It boggles me that as unusual of a town as Moon Grove is, its citizens don't seem to be particularly open-minded."

"Well, that leads me to my next question. Hypothetically, is there any way one of these tonics you're selling could be used by someone to, say, start a fire?" I asked.

Hilda's expression darkened. "I couldn't rule it out. While I've obviously not tested my products for unintended uses, I can say they're all safe and non-combustible in their packaged forms.

However, I suppose it's possible for a particularly talented witch or warlock to reverse engineer the formula or extract certain contents," Hilda said.

Bingo. I still wasn't convinced Hypnotic Tonics had nothing to do with what happened to Circe, but at least I had something else to look at now. I'd seen enough in my time in Moon Grove to know there was no limit to some people's creativity — if it could be called that.

"But I want to be clear: I would never willingly sell anything that wasn't safe. Sage and I went through chaos to get the store open, and I don't want to do anything that might jeopardize it. This is my life's work, Zoe. I'm sure you understand," Hilda said.

Either she was telling the truth or she was a very convincing actress — I couldn't tell which. Though I considered popping into her thoughts to verify, I thought better of it. If she was talented enough of a witch to brew all these tonics, Lilith only knew what else she was capable of doing.

Besides, if she was lying, it would come out in the stir eventually. The proof might literally be in the potion.

"Understood. One last question," I started. Hilda raised an eyebrow at me.

"Yes?"

"I noticed that all the tonics in your case have the same symbol etched into their stoppers. What is it?" I asked. Hilda smiled.

"It's an ancient alchemical symbol," she said. "The All-Seeing Eye. It's meant to symbolize how alchemy, potions, and tonics can help us open our Third Eye to things outside our realm we couldn't normally see."

Or, you know, crazed hallucinations. Same difference.

"How inspiring," I said, and Hilda's smile widened. "Well, thank you both very much for your time. I'll be in touch if I have any follow up questions for the article," I said, unsure of how true that was.

"Of course. I can't wait to see what you come up with, Zoe. I've heard you have a magical way with words," Hilda said.

I also had a magical way of finding the truth, so she'd better be careful what she wished for with me.

"I hope it's good after all this," Sage mumbled, and Hilda narrowed her eyes at her.

"Oh, it will be, don't you worry about that," I said and showed myself out of the shop.

CHAPTER SEVEN

AFTER TRANSCRIBING my thoughts on my chat with Hilda and Sage, I decided to call it a day and pay a visit to Raina and Grandma Elle. I hadn't seen either of them since my mock trial with the Council and if I knew grandma half as well as I thought it did, she was probably be coming unglued worrying about me.

I didn't bother heading home first. Instead, I continued north on Crescent Street past Swiftsage and Flora's house to Moonbeam Lane — and froze at the intersection, unable to go any further.

Images of the raging green fire flashed in my mind and as much as I tried not to, my eyes locked on the end of the street where Circe's house used to stand. How could I face Raina after this and the way she'd come to my rescue during my grilling by the Council?

I would just have to try. There wasn't any other way around it.

With a sigh, I gathered myself and continued down Moonbeam to number three. As I passed the other small brick homes that lined the street, it occurred to me I'd become an entirely different person since I'd last been to Raina's house. Hardly any time at all had passed, but so much had happened in that short few weeks.

Raina's small brick cottage was as unassuming yet inviting as ever. Now that I thought about it, it seemed perfect as a house for someone like my grandmother, which gave me hope Elle was comfortable inside. I didn't quite understand why the Council wanted Grandma to stay in Moon Grove after the fit they threw about me bringing her there in the first place, but I wasn't complaining.

I knocked gently on the door, careful not to surprise either of them. At first, no one answered, but a few seconds later I heard stirring from inside. Raina opened the door and gave me a smile, though it wasn't a particularly warm one.

"I was wondering when we might see you," she said.

"Hey, I'm sorry I didn't ask ahead of time. I just got off work and, well, I needed to decompress," I said.

"No need to explain, dear," she said and stepped aside. I maneuvered around her and found Grandma Elle sitting in the largest of three rocking chairs by the fireplace in the cozy living room. Tierney, Raina's cranky and fluffy tabby cat, sat purring in Grandma's lap — something I didn't know the cat was capable of doing.

I didn't know which was more shocking: the fact that Grandma let a cat get anywhere near her or the fact that Tierney seemed to like her.

"No way," I said, staring at the two of them with my eyes wide open to make sure I wasn't dreaming.

"I couldn't believe it either," Raina laughed as she closed the door and joined us in the living room. "As you found out your first time here, Tierney has trouble with new people, so there must be something special about your grandmother. I've never seen Tierney take to someone so quickly."

"Please. Ain't nothing special about this old crone," Grandma said and I laughed. Seeing her there with Tierney in her lap was surreal, a physical manifestation of my two very different worlds colliding. But as unbelievable as it was, somehow Grandma fit in perfectly — and I didn't ever want her to leave.

"None of us believes that for a second," I said, cautiously sitting in one of the smaller rocking chairs next to Grandma to avoid scaring Tierney, but the cat seemed oblivious as Grandma continued to scratch the top of his head.

"That's true. You raised Zoe, so you must have a Herculean amount of patience," Raina said and Grandma cackled.

"Oh, you ain't got *no* idea," Grandma said.

"Well, it seems like the two of you are getting along without a hitch," I said, rolling my eyes.

"Arguably, she's doing a better job of adjusting than you did, Zoe," Raina said.

"That doesn't surprise me. She's always had more grit and resilience than I have," I said.

"A lifetime of breakin' your back plantin' seeds in cow dung will do that fer a girl," Grandma said. "I swear, Raina, I always tried to get Zoe to spend more time on the farm for that reason, but she wasn't havin' it. The lil' devil couldn't stand the feelin' of dirt under her nails."

"That was probably good for both of us, in retrospect. I've killed pretty much every plant I've touched," I said and Grandma smiled at me.

"Yeah, I reckon you're right. Anyway, how you been, Sugar? You holdin' it together?"

"As well as can be expected, I guess," I said with a shrug.

"Why don't I make us some tea and we can talk everything over?" Raina suggested and I nodded.

"So long as you ain't gonna catch on fire too, sounds good to me," Grandma said. "I swear, I got me a bad case of PTSD or whatever it's called after this whole thing."

"Don't worry, I've cast every protective spell I can think of over this home. It's fireproof," Raina said from the kitchen as she rustled in the cupboards for her ingredients — an interesting choice considering she normally used magic to make tea. Maybe she figured Grandma had seen enough magic lately.

"That's good to hear," I said, and I meant it. As much as I tried to keep it out of my mind, every now and then the fear of something happening to Grandma crept into the corners of my consciousness like an unwelcome spider.

The conversation died as Raina occupied herself with the tea, and had it not been for the sound of Tierney's motor-like purring, silence would've swallowed us.

"Zoe, dear, I'm sorry about your wand revoking and suspension from Veilside," Raina said as she came back into the living room with three steaming mugs magically floating in front of her. Without thinking, I took two out of the air and handed one to Grandma.

"Floatin' mugs, fer Chrissakes. I ain't ever gonna get used to this place," Grandma sighed. "I don't suppose y'all have a church around here anywhere do you?"

"No, I'm sorry to say we don't. Perhaps unsurprisingly, the residents here have no need for something like that," Raina said as she eased down into the third rocking chair beside Grandma

"Can't blame a girl for askin'," Grandma said.

"It's okay, Raina, I didn't take it personally," I said, ignoring Grandma and her kooky commentary. "Honestly, the punishment could've been much worse — and probably should've been."

"You're lucky, that's for certain," Raina said and sipped her tea. I followed suit, letting the warmth and spice flow through me. I wasn't sure what kind of tea it was, but it was delicious.

"It's an herbal tea. No caffeine and no magical properties," Raina said as if she'd read my mind. Grandma stopped just short of tipping back her mug.

"So just to be sure, this ain't gonna make me grow hair where the sun don't shine, right?" Grandma asked and Raina smiled, amused.

"No, no worries about that. It's the same sort of tea you might drink back home," Raina said.

"Good. Ain't nothin' wrong with keepin' things traditional," Grandma said and took a healthy swig. "Somethin' tells me y'all need some more tradition around here."

"We have numerous traditions of our own here in Moon Grove, Mrs. Clark. As a matter of fact, you may get to see them first hand soon," Raina said and turned to me. "Which reminds me, Zoe, I don't know if you've heard, but we've arranged funeral services for Circe on Sunday morning," Raina continued and I froze.

"That's, uh, good to hear, but I don't know if it's appropriate for me to attend," I said, my cheeks flaring. More than that, I wasn't sure I could handle it. Everyone would no doubt stare and whisper about me — not that that was uncommon for me these days — but it still made me want to crawl out of my skin.

"I understand, but I wanted to extend the invitation anyway. If you change your mind, of course, you're welcome to join us," Raina said.

"Us?"

"Don't be dense, Sugar. I'm gonna be there too," Grandma said.

"Oh, okay. Good for you," I said, unsure of what else to say. Somehow, I didn't see that playing well in the eyes of the Council and everyone else who seemingly was convinced my grandmother and I had something to do with the death of Circe, but what did I know?

"You all right? Rough day at the office?" Grandma asked.

"Yeah, I'm fine, just got a lot on my mind," I said and Grandma narrowed her eyes at me.

"It's a darn good thing you're in the business of getting other people to tell the truth because you couldn't lie to save your life," Grandma said and Raina smirked at me. She wasn't wrong.

"Go on then, spit it out. It's rarer than Moonshine for the cat to get hold of your tongue and keep it," Grandma said.

"It's about Circe," I started, watching Raina's face for a reaction. The smile vanished, but she nodded to tell me to continue.

"I haven't told anyone this yet, or at least not anyone important, but I found something at Circe's house the night she died," I said. Both Grandma and Raina eyed me.

"You ain't gotta be so cagey," Grandma said.

"She's right," Raina said, the beginnings of a smile returning to her face.

"Well, it's probably easier for me just to show it to you," I said and reached into the pocket of my robes for the vial stopper. I held it out in my palm and rolled it so the symbol of the open eye pointed upward.

"What in tarnation is that?" Grandma asked, squinting.

"The All-Seeing Eye," Raina said, recognizing the symbol immediately. Well, that certainly made Hilda seem far less suspicious. Maybe she really was telling the truth about the symbol.

"Yeah, that's what the owner of Hypnotic Tonics told me too," I said.

"That sounds to me like you don't believe it," Raina said.

"I'm not sure, honestly," I said. "It just seems odd to me that I'd find this little guy near a crime scene. I don't think it's a stretch to wonder if it was some sort of potion or tonic that caused the fire."

"I see," Raina said as she swirled the tea in her mug.

"What're you tryin' to say, Sugar? You think somebody did this on purpose?" Grandma asked.

"They must have. Magical fires like that one don't start on accident, and I don't know if it's possible for a witch or warlock to cast the kind of spell that would lead to a blaze like that one," I said. Raina nodded.

"It is possible, though highly unlikely," she said. "A fire that large and intense would require the magic of more than one witch or warlock."

As the Headmistress of one of the most prestigious magical schools in the world, I was inclined to take her word for it.

"That's sort of what I thought. Besides, how likely is it that several witches and warlocks would be able to band together to light a house on fire during a town-wide curfew without being noticed?" I asked.

"Well, you managed to subvert the curfew without being caught, so it's not impossible. A witch or warlock with the appropriate spells could have made themselves temporarily invisible, though I would hope the Council accounted for things like that in preparation for the curfew," Raina said.

"Now wait a hot second," Grandma said. "Now that you mention it, I think I saw somethin' or somebody out there lurkin' around that night."

I sat bolt upright in the rocking chair so fast it jerked Tierney out of his dead sleep. He hissed at me, but grandma continued scratching his head and he settled.

"Why are you just now telling me this?!" I asked.

"Well, I wasn't a hundred percent sure and I didn't want to lead nobody down an empty rabbit hole," Grandma said.

"This is serious, Grandma. What did you see?" I asked, shuddering at the thought of what it might've been. Given we were under the curfew for the effects of the Blood Moon that night, it could very well have been a rogue werewolf who'd caught her foreign scent — or worse.

"I couldn't make it out real clear because Circe had all the drapes pulled shut tighter than purse strings, but I know I saw *somethin'* moving out there while Circe wasn't lookin'," Grandma said.

"What did it look like? Was it big, small, human, hairy?"

"I dunno, I really don't. All I know is I saw somethin' or somebody outside that window just a few minutes before the place went up in flames," Grandma said.

"A few minutes before? So it wasn't immediately before the house caught on fire?" I asked.

"No, it was at least two or three minutes before that. I didn't think nothin' of it at first, but I saw somethin' movin' outta the corner of my eye and that's when I started payin' more attention," Grandma said.

"But then it stopped and I figured it was just one of the trees surroundin' the place swayin' in the breeze and playin' tricks on me," she continued. "That's why I never said nothin'. I can't be sure."

"But you don't think it was just a tree, do you?" Raina asked.

"I mean, it mighta been, but I never seen a tree move that fast in all my life," Grandma said. A chill ran down my spine.

"You probably knew her better than anyone else, Raina. Did Circe have any political enemies who might've wanted to hurt her?" I asked. Raina's expression darkened and she stared down into her tea as if she were trying to read the future in its surface.

"I can't answer that directly, but I do know that my dear sister was involved in some tense negotiations," Raina said. "I didn't want to believe that said negotiations could have anything to do with her death, but given our lack of answers, it can't be ruled out."

"Who was she working with and why were their talks tense?" I asked.

"After what happened to Opal Cromwell, Circe made it a personal mission to reach out and negotiate with the various paranormal groups in Moon Grove to try to improve relations on behalf of the Council," Raina said. "But her primary focus was with the werewolves."

All the blood drained from my face. It couldn't have been a coincidence that Circe died on the same night a seemingly arbitrary curfew was placed on the entire town thanks to the Blood Moon — which allegedly affected werewolves more than anyone else in town.

"Why? As far as I know, she doesn't have any connections to the werewolves."

"It was more out of necessity than desire, at least according to her," Raina said. "After the vampires made their power known, other groups in town took notice and decided they wanted to make a play for power as well. The werewolves were no exception."

Yet again, I felt like I'd run into an unintended consequence of my own actions.

"But where the vampires preferred to operate in the shadows, literally and figuratively, the werewolves were much more aggressive and direct in their approach. They lobbied the Council daily, and for whatever reason, Circe was their main influence target," Raina continued.

If I had to venture a guess, it was probably because the werewolves thought Circe would be more of a pushover than anyone else on the Council. They were wrong, and maybe that was what led to her death.

"That implies she wasn't the only one they talked to, though. Who else?" I asked.

"Lorelei Riddle," Raina said, her voice so low I barely heard her.

That made two connections. So not only had Lorelei given Hilda a hex of a time getting her shop up and running, but she was also connected to Circe via their respective interactions with the werewolves.

"I shouldn't be surprised, but I am," I said, reeling.

"Y'all sound like you're writin' an episode of *Game of Thrones* with all this political mumbo-jumbo," Grandma said. She wasn't far off the mark.

"Sorry, we must be boring you to death," I said.

"Far from it. I feel like I'm right smack dab in the middle of a TV show. All I need's some butter-laden, artery-cloggin' popcorn," Grandma said.

"Sorry to spoil the fun, but I should probably get going," I said. Grandma frowned.

"Get goin'? Girl, you just got here!"

"I know, but I've got a lot to of new info to chew on," I said.

"All right, have it your way," Grandma said.

"Let us know if there's anything we can do to help, Zoe," Raina said. "In the meantime, I think it would be wise to spend this time together with your grandmother getting to the bottom of your family's origins."

"Sounds good," I said, though I thought the opposite. Raina smirked, seeing right through me.

"Don't go doin' nothin' crazy now, Sugar," Grandma said as I stood. She reached for my hand and squeezed it in hers. "Now that I'm here, I don't want anything to happen to you. I'd never be able to forgive myself."

"I'll be fine, I always am. I love you, Gram. Stay out of trouble," I said and kissed the back of Grandma's hand.

"Trouble? Me? Never," Grandma said, smiling.

Raina stood and walked me to the door. I opened it and stepped outside.

"Be careful, Zoe," Raina said, clutching the handle. For the first time I could remember, she seemed shaken, frightened — but she had every reason to be. She'd lost more people in the last few weeks than anyone ever deserved.

"I will, I promise. I know she's a handful, but thank you for taking my grandma in and keeping her safe," I said.

"Of course, dear," she said, wearing a sad smile. "Good luck with Lorelei."

"Same to you," I said and Raina closed the door, leaving me with a sinking feeling.

As much as I wanted to avoid it, I didn't have a choice anymore. It was time to pay another unexpected, almost certainly unwanted visit to a Council member — whose daughter I'd recently put behind bars.

So much for a quiet weekend.

CHAPTER EIGHT

THE SATURDAY SUN rose with a vengeance and I wasn't ready to face it. All night long I'd tossed and turned thinking about Grandma, the Council, and how on Earth I was supposed to talk to Lorelei Riddle without getting cursed by her in the process.

It seemed like I was never going to get caught up on my sleep.

Annoyed, I rolled out of bed and shuffled into the living room to find Flora sitting on the couch bright-eyed and sparkly winged. She held the Saturday edition of The Moon Grove Messenger in one hand and a steaming mug of coffee in the other.

"You're up awfully early," she said without looking at me. Her eyes darted across the page as she finished whatever she was reading.

"Not by choice," I sighed. "Where's Luna?"

"Still in my bed," Flora said and set the paper down on the couch beside her.

"I swear, she might as well not even be my cat anymore," I said and Flora smiled.

"She told me you were flailing around too much for her liking last night," Flora said.

"Well, we wouldn't want to disturb the diva of the house, would we?" I asked. "Is there any coffee left?"

"Plenty. It's still in the carafe," Flora said. I went into the kitchen and scoured the cupboards for the biggest mug I could find. The coffee bubbled and gurgled as I poured it and the smell alone made me feel a little better.

"Wait, since when do you read our paper when you aren't working on it?" I called.

"I don't get to see everything before it's printed, you know," Flora called back. "I only edit what Mitch puts on my desk."

"Fair enough," I said as I came back into the living room and sat down beside her. "Anything good? I mean, besides my pieces?"

"No one could hold a wand to you," Flora said, smiling.

"Good answer."

"What are your plans today?"

"Oh, you know, just another typical Saturday spent crashing a Councilwoman's house. Nothing out of the ordinary," I said. Flora chuckled.

"Who's the lucky one this time?"

"Lorelei Riddle," I said, grimacing.

"Are you serious?" Flora whispered.

"Yes, as much as I wish I wasn't," I said.

"Why?"

"Turns out she and Circe Woods have more in common than I realized," I said. "I went to visit Raina and my grandma last night and Raina told me both Circe and Lorelei have been lobbied by the werewolves."

"Yikes," Flora said. "For what?"

"I dunno, but I'd guess the same thing everyone lobbies for: power," I said, shrugging.

"Do you really think she'll talk to you after what happened between you and Aurelia?" Flora asked.

"There's only one way to find out, and I've learned that showing up unannounced gets the best results," I said and Flora frowned.

"How long do you think you'll be?" she asked.

"No clue, but probably not too long. Why?" I asked.

"Well, I'm going out with Ewan tonight so I thought you and Beau might like to join us since our last attempt was—"

"An unqualified disaster, yeah, I remember," I interrupted. Flora had invited us out on a double date with her on-again, off-again werewolf boyfriend, Officer Ewan Barrett — but I'd run off shoeless in the middle of it to chase after the magical medics.

"That's not what I was going to say."

"But you were thinking it," I said.

Flora shrugged. "Maybe."

"As much as I'd like to go, it's probably best if you two have the night to yourselves," I said. "Besides, I'm not sure where Beau and I stand right now."

"What does that mean?" Flora asked.

"I haven't seen or spoken to him since the Council took my wand away," I said. "He hasn't called or anything."

"You know the phone works both ways, right?" Flora asked.

"Very funny. I dunno, I just… I have a lot on my plate right now and I don't think he's particularly thrilled with me for what I did, as supportive as he was during the aftermath," I said.

"Are you sure that isn't just your own negativity making things up?" Flora asked.

"It probably is, but that's another reason I should keep some space between us for a while, or at least until this all blows over," I said. "Everyone knows we're dating and what I did probably isn't helping him look good in the public eye."

"Somehow, I don't think he cares much about that," Flora said. "Promise me you'll call him when you're done with Lorelei?"

"Yes, big sis," I sighed, rolling my eyes. Smiling, Flora leaned over and pulled me into a hug.

"I know this hasn't been easy, but don't beat yourself up, Zoe. You've got plenty of friends and supporters around here, including Beau and me," Flora said.

"Well, since you're so eager to help, do you have any idea where Lorelei lives?" I asked. Flora glared at me.

"That wasn't the kind of help I had in mind," she said as she let go of me.

"But it's the kind I need," I said.

"You're a journalist, you ought to know how to look someone up by now," Flora said.

"Sure I do, but it's more fun to ask you to do it for me," I said. Flora laughed and shook her head.

"Fine. I'm sure she's in the Parapages just like everyone else," she said and waved her hand. An intimidating tome with a spine as tall as a cinder brick drifted out from under the coffee table and into Flora's lap.

"How do they keep this thing updated anyway? It seems like it'd be a massive headache," I said.

"Magic, of course. How else?" Flora asked.

"Right, duh, silly me." Apparently, there wasn't anything in Moon Grove done by hand if magic could do the job instead.

With another wave of Flora's hand, the directory flipped itself to the surname entries starting with the letter R. Flora skimmed through a few pages until she stabbed her finger into the book.

"A-ha. There," she said. I followed her finger to an entry that said "Devon and Lorelei Riddle, 12 Amethyst Street, Witches' Quarter."

My whole body seized. That meant Lorelei lived on the street right behind Circe. Though it could've been nothing more than a coincidence, I didn't like the optics one bit.

If a klutz like me could sneak undetected through Moon Grove during a mandatory curfew, it wouldn't have taken much at all for an advanced witch like Lorelei to sneak through the alley separating her house from Circe's — or simply lob a highly flammable potion from the cover of the shadows.

Grandma *did* say she saw something moving outside.

"Zoe?" Flora asked, and I snapped out of my thoughts.

"What? Sorry," I said.

"I asked what you were going to do."

"Oh, good question. I'll probably just go over there and see what happens. The worst Lorelei can do is slam the door in my face," I said. "It's not like that's never happened to me before."

"Ah, the life of a reporter. I don't miss that at all," Flora said.

"It isn't all bad. I get to talk to lots of, erm, 'colorful' characters," I said. "Anyway, I better get moving."

"Be careful," Flora said as I got off the couch.

"You say that all the time and yet…"

"Don't remind me," Flora sighed.

"Thanks for the help," I said.

"Don't mention it," Flora said. "No, seriously, don't."

"You got it," I said and left to take a shower, hoping the hot water would calm my racing brain. Unfortunately, as good as it felt, it didn't have the desired effect. All I could think about was Lorelei and her possible links to Circe's death.

Still in a tizzy mentally, I got dressed and slung my bag over my shoulder on my way out the door, wishing I had a wand to take with me even if I didn't have a clue how to do anything useful with it. It was more of a security blanket than anything. Regardless, by the time I walked across town to the intersection of Crescent and Amethyst, I wished I hadn't.

What exactly was I supposed to say to Lorelei while I stood there on her doorstep? I doubted something along the lines of "Hey, Councilwoman, I think you might've had something to do with the death of your colleague because you live near her" would cut it.

But there wasn't any turning back now, so I set off down Amethyst Street toward number twelve. The houses along the way looked more or less like the rest in the Witches' Quarter: small, made of brick, and characteristically quirky in their decorations.

Lorelei's home wasn't any different, minus the number of potted plants that littered her front porch and the accompanying garden beneath the front windows bursting with color. Thanks to her icy personality, I wouldn't have taken Lorelei for a gardener — Moon Grove really was full of endless surprises.

With a lump in my throat, I walked among the flora lining the pathway to the front door and racked my brain for something to say. I really needed to come up with a better strategy than showing up at people's houses, but it didn't matter because as I raised my hand to knock, the door swung open.

"Dear Lilith," Lorelei gasped, clutching her chest. "Zoe, what are you doing here? You scared me half to death."

"Sorry, I was just about to knock when you opened," I said, my hand still raised to prove it.

"Who's there?" a male voice called from inside.

"No one, dear, don't worry about it," Lorelei called back over her shoulder, her voice like honey. She stepped outside and closed the door and immediately her face soured. "What do you want?" she asked, her tone back to acidic.

"I have a few questions I want to ask you," I said. Lorelei narrowed her eyes at me and crossed her arms over her chest.

"You could've called," she said. "Or made an appointment to speak to me during office hours."

"I know, but somehow I didn't think you'd accept," I said. Lorelei scoffed.

"If it's nothing to do with business, I don't have anything to say to you," Lorelei said and whirled on her heel to go back inside.

"Councilwoman, wait," I called after, but she slammed the door in my face — as expected. Sighing, I stood unsure of what to do. I hadn't come all this way for nothing, but getting anything out of Lorelei would obviously be a chore. Tenacity was the only way through.

I pounded on the door, much more forcefully than was necessary, and waited. She couldn't ignore me forever, and I'd knock all day if she forced me. Who knew, if I annoyed her enough, she might let slip something she would never have said otherwise.

"Are you out of your mind?" Lorelei shouted as she flung the door open again. "I should have you arrested for harassment."

"Harassment is probably somewhere in my job description, Councilwoman," I said. "If we journalists didn't pester our representatives, they'd never tell us anything."

"This is no time for your humor, Ms. Clarke," Lorelei said. "Now leave before I call the police. If you want to talk to me, do it through the proper channels and contact my staff."

She made to slam the door again, but I wedged my foot in between it and the doorframe. The heavy wood smashed my foot so hard I thought it was going to explode and it took everything I had not to shriek, but I refused to let her see me in pain so I bit it back.

"You really are out of your mind," Lorelei laughed, but she seemed impressed more than anything else.

"No, just determined. Don't forget, Councilwoman, you're an elected representative and you're supposed to serve me," I said. Lorelei fixed me with a look that said she would gladly have cursed me to hex and back if she could have but thought better of it.

"What in Lilith's name is going on out there?" the male voice called again and I heard footsteps coming down the hall toward the door. Lorelei sighed, looking defeated.

"Fine. Five minutes, no more," she said and flung the door open. Cautiously, I stepped around her inside and came face-to-face with a handsome man her age whose hands were covered in soil. If he was the one responsible for the plants it would've explained why they hadn't all withered and died already under Lorelei's care.

"Oh, hello," the man said. "I'm Devon, Lorelei's husband. I'd offer you a hand, but well," he said, raising his dirty hands.

"Zoe Clarke, and no worries," I said, barely acknowledging him. Once he realized who I was, I had a feeling all his hospitality would run out of his ears. He looked me up and down like he recognized my name but couldn't figure out where from until at last it dawned on him.

"Oh, you were one of Aurelia's classmates, weren't you?" Devon asked with much more grace than I deserved.

"Yeah, something like that," I said.

"We were just on our way out," Lorelei said.

"I won't keep you. I just wanted to ask you a couple of questions about Councilwoman Woods," I said and Lorelei's face darkened.

"I don't think that's appropriate, Ms. Clarke," Lorelei said.

"She's just doing her job, Lorelei," Devon muttered. He wasn't wrong. The sooner she answered my questions, the sooner I would leave. And if she refused to answer, I'd just keep asking until she did — today or four days from now.

"Make it quick, we have people waiting on us," Lorelei snapped.

"Please, come in, sit down," Devon said, waving me into the living room from the hall. Lorelei looked like her head was going to shoot off of her shoulders like a burst berry. The last thing I wanted to do was get comfortable in Lorelei Riddle's home, but it wasn't like I could say no.

"It's okay, don't be afraid," Devon said, clearly unfazed. Reluctantly, I followed him down the hall and into the living room, which was cozy but not unbearably so. The walls were painted a powder blue — and were lined with photos of Aurelia and her grandmother, Claudette, the previous head witch of Moon Grove.

Mr. Riddle gestured for me to sit on the plush white leather sofa and I couldn't refuse his hospitality, so I sat. He washed his hands in the kitchen sink and Lorelei sat directly across from me in one of the two matching chairs.

Everywhere I looked, Aurelia's too-perfect blue eyes and beautiful blonde hair stared back, taunting me. It was a surreal experience to look at photos of someone I'd sent to jail less than two weeks prior while having a casual conversation with her parents, yet there I was.

But the strangest thing was that Lorelei herself wasn't in any of the pictures. Devon appeared here and there, but Lorelei was nowhere to be found. I made a mental note of that, not sure if it meant anything.

"Look, I know this is awkward, but I swear I'm not trying to make it that way," I said, unable to bear the silence that had fallen between us after I sat. "I'm only here because I don't know who else to ask."

"It's okay, we had a feeling you might be dropping by at some point," Devon said as he joined us. Oh, really? Why was that? As much as I wanted to know, I decided not to ask.

"Okay. Well, I guess I'll just get right to it then," I said, shrugging. "I heard through the grapevine that both you and Councilwoman Woods were involved in some sort of negotiations with the werewolves. Is that true?"

Though Lorelei gulped, she nodded to confirm.

"It is," she said, refusing to look me in the eye.

"What sort of negotiations were they?" I asked.

"Standard negotiations, nothing out of the ordinary. Since the vampires got a stake in their heart to gain some influence with the Council, the werewolves decided they didn't want to be left out. We were just trying to contain the situation," Lorelei said.

"What situation?" I asked. Lorelei sighed and brought her hand to her forehead.

"You're digging for something that isn't there, Ms. Clarke. This is a non-starter of a story," she said.

"Maybe it is, but one of your colleagues just died in a house fire, so I don't think you can blame me for asking," I said. It was probably too forceful, but I had already taken enough off of Lorelei in the last few days — I couldn't do it anymore.

"And you think I had something to do with it, is that what you're saying?" Lorelei asked. "That's absurd. You can ask Devon, I was home that night, just like everyone else *should* have been," she continued. It was an obvious dig about me breaking the curfew, but I ignored it.

"It's true, she was here cooking dinner when the fire broke out. We didn't know about it until much later that night when Heath called," Devon said.

"Thank you, dear. Look, Ms. Clarke, I know you probably think Aurelia must've learned to murder from me, but let me be clear: I would *never* dream of harming another witch," Lorelei said. "What Aurelia did to Professor Frost, it's... it's unspeakable. She's far too ambitious for her own good, always has been. Ambition may run in the Riddle family, but not like that."

Ambitious probably wasn't the word I would've chosen to describe Lorelei's daughter, but it still wasn't inaccurate. Cutthroat might've been better, though — literally and figuratively.

"And what about you, Mrs. Riddle? Are you ambitious?" I asked. She narrowed her eyes at me.

"Implying what, exactly?"

"Nothing, it was a straightforward question. You're the newest witch on Moon Grove's Council and I'm sure you didn't get there by resting on your laurels," I said.

"I didn't murder anyone for the job and I certainly wouldn't kill a colleague to boost my profile if that's what you're suggesting," Lorelei said.

"I wasn't suggesting anything, but okay. Anyway, one last question and I'll get out of your hair," I said.

"Right on time. Your five minutes are almost over," Lorelei said, smiling.

"I spoke to Hilda Blackwood yesterday," I said and Lorelei's smile fell from her face like rain from the sky. "She told me that you more than anyone else on the Council gave her and her shop quite a bit of trouble when she was trying to get approval to open it. Why's that?"

"Lilith, what a PR disaster this has become," Lorelei said under breath. "I'm only going to say this one more time for the record: I don't and have never had any interest in using my position to antagonize Hilda or anyone else."

"Not even if they're dirty hippies?" I asked and Lorelei's face twisted. Zing!

"Every day I regret saying that more," she sighed, but I wasn't buying it. Lorelei probably didn't regret saying it so much as she regretted it being spread. "Despite that, I assure you I don't have any bias against Hilda or her shop. I only wanted to make sure we weren't introducing unforeseen dangers into the community via unregulated substances."

Yeah, right.

"That's not what Sage Snow told me," I said. Lorelei's frown deepened.

"Somehow, I'm not surprised to hear that," she said.

"Why?"

"I'm not in the business of gossiping so I'll leave it at this: if I were you, I'd be paying close attention to Ms. Snow," Lorelei said. "As, erm, *eccentric* as Hilda is, not even she can hold a tie-dyed candle to Sage's brand of quirky."

"Being quirky doesn't make you a criminal," I said. If that were true, everyone in Moon Grove would be behind bars.

"You're right, it doesn't. But I swear to you, Ms. Clarke, there's something not quite trustworthy about her," Lorelei said.

As a member of the Council, Lorelei probably knew more about every citizen in town than I ever would, but I wasn't sure I believed her about Sage. She seemed pretty normal to me; maybe a little peeved about the way the Council had treated her and Hilda, but I would've been too if it were me.

"Don't forget, she's Hilda's apprentice. She has access to everything inside that shop: the tonics, the ingredients, the formulas, everything. And thanks to Hilda's instruction, Sage knows how to use them too," Lorelei continued.

A chill swept over me. I hadn't thought about that. I'd been so fixated on Hilda at the time that I didn't even consider Sage as a culprit. She had access to the weapons, and she definitely had a motive, though I would've guessed she'd go after Lorelei before Circe. Still, maybe anyone on the Council was good enough...

"Between you and me, I've heard she has a certain proclivity for fire in her studies," Lorelei said, snapping me out of my thoughts. So much for avoiding gossip, but I wasn't complaining. It was good information to have, as frightening as it was.

"I see. Well, thanks for your time, Mr. and Mrs. Riddle," I said as I stood from the sofa, careful not to look at any of the photos of Aurelia on the walls.

"It was our pleasure," Mr. Riddle said, standing to offer me a hand to shake. What was his deal? I put his daughter in jail and more or less accused his wife of murder too, so why was he being so nice to me? It was almost like he was grateful to be rid of Aurelia.

I placed my hand in his, shook it twice, and quickly withdrew. Lorelei stood but crossed her arms over her chest. Clearly, she didn't echo her husband's sentiment.

"I'll walk you out," Lorelei said, gesturing toward the front door for me to lead and I didn't dare argue. As we walked, I felt her eyes laser-focused on my back and didn't stop thinking about all the ways she could curse me into oblivion until my hand met the cold metal of the doorknob.

I flung it open and stepped outside never more grateful for fresh air. When I turned around, Lorelei stared at me flat faced.

"I'm sorry I interrupted your plans," I lied. She scoffed.

"So am I. Don't ever come here unannounced again, Ms. Clarke. I won't be so nice about it next time," Lorelei said and slammed the door shut in my face.

As far as I was concerned, there wouldn't be another.

CHAPTER NINE

MY PHONE VIBRATED on the couch beside me, making me jump up from the notes I'd been taking. Grateful for the distraction, I picked up the phone and smiled when I saw I had a message from Mallory.

>>*Mallory: Hey, what are you up to today?*

Though I had a ton on my mind and even more work to do making sense of all the info I'd gathered, I didn't know where to go with any of it. Mallory could be a good person to bounce my ideas off in the meantime.

>>*Me: Not much, trying to make sense of everything I've learned in the last couple days. What about you? Anything new on the picture I sent you?*

>> *Mallory: Actually, that's why I'm writing. Can I come over?*

>>*Me: Yeah, sure. I'm just sitting around pretending like I'm working anyway.*

>>*Mallory: Okay, I'll be there in a few minutes. Brace yourself.*

>>*Me: I always do when you're around.*

Mallory didn't answer, which I assumed meant she didn't find my joke very funny, but she was difficult to offend so I wasn't worried. True to her word, she knocked on the door just a few minutes later and I wondered if she flew there — or if she was already on my street when she texted.

I climbed off the couch and let Mallory inside. Without a word, she strode past me in a blur of emerald robes and brown hair to flop on the couch, her nest of hair bouncing along with her.

"Nice to see you again too," I laughed, closing the door behind her.

"Sorry, I ran here in a hurry, I'm exhausted," she said.

"It must've been important then. What did you find out? I only ask because I might already have an answer, but I'm curious what you learned," I said.

"That symbol you sent me seems to have a couple of different meanings, depending on who you ask," Mallory said through her heaving breaths.

"Really? As far as I knew, it only had one meeting. Both Raina and Hilda told me it's what's known as the All-Seeing Eye, which I guess is some sort of alchemical thing," I said.

"That's true, but like I said, there are other meanings," Mallory said.

"I don't like the sound of this. The last time you did research on a symbol for me, you stirred up all kinds of things I could've gone the rest of my life without knowing," I said, remembering with dread that I had distant familial links to the founder of one of Moon Grove's oldest cults, the Black Brotherhood.

"Well, don't drop your broom just yet, it's not that serious," Mallory said.

"Okay, then what is it?"

"That eye is also associated with, erm, hippies," Mallory said and I laughed. That definitely lined up with my impression of Hilda and Sage and explained why they'd taken the symbol as their shop's logo.

"That fits based on what I know now," I said.

"Yeah, but that's the weird thing. No matter how much I looked, I couldn't figure out why they picked that symbol in particular," Mallory said.

"Maybe they just liked the way it looked. Not everything has to be some grand conspiracy, you know?" I asked.

"Heresy!" Mallory said and I laughed. "In the world of research, there's no such thing as coincidences."

"Well in the real world where the rest of us live, there is," I said as I sat down beside her.

"Were you taking some sort of notes?" Mallory asked, nodding at the notebook I'd left open on the couch.

"I was writing down some thoughts and observations I had about the people I've talked to in the last couple of days," I said.

"Let me guess: you're chasing after whoever killed Councilwoman Woods, aren't you?" Mallory asked.

"How can you know me so well in such a short amount of time?"

"You're not exactly subtle," Mallory said. "I swear, murder seems to follow you. You're cursed or something,"

"I hope you aren't right about that," I sighed.

"Probably not. Where's Flora?"

"Good question, I haven't seen her all morning. When I woke up she wasn't here. I know she went on a date with her boyfriend last night, so maybe she never came home," I said.

"Oh, how scandalous! I love it," Mallory said, rubbing her hands together like some sort of diabolical mastermind. "Speaking of scandals, who all have you talked to already?"

"I started with Hilda Blackwood, the owner of that new alchemical store, Hypnotic Tonics," I said and Mallory raised an eyebrow at me.

"Why?"

"Well, I didn't send you that picture of the symbol for no reason. I'm sure you've already heard by now, but I made the mistake of trying to sneak my grandmother into Moon Grove and it didn't work out in my favor," I said.

"Seriously, girl, what were you thinking?" Mallory asked.

"I wasn't," I said.

"Fair enough. So, what's the connection then? Why go talk to Hilda?"

"I found a vial stopper outside Circe's house during the fire. Well, more accurately, I tripped on it. Anyway, I don't think it was a coincidence that it was there, which is why I sent you the picture to help figure out where it might've come from," I said. Mallory nodded.

"But I didn't put two and two together until I showed the stopper to Mitch, my boss over at the Messenger, and he tipped me off about Hypnotic Tonics. It made sense because the flames that burned Circe's house to the ground were definitely magical."

"Yeah, I read about that in the paper," Mallory said.

"Actually, I'm glad you're here because I've been meaning to ask you what you think about it. I've never heard of any sort of fire that burns green, have you?" I asked. Of course I hadn't, I hadn't grown up in Moon Grove where up was down and down was up.

"I mean, of course I had to go digging as soon as I read about it," Mallory said.

"Yeah, I suspected," I said. Mallory smirked at me. "What did you find?"

"Well, it's a bit of a mystery how it's made according to what I read, but still, the only thing that fits the description is this stuff I found in an old Alchemy textbook of mine called Wild Fyre. That's fire with a Y," Mallory said.

"Wait, why do they spell it with a Y? And how can they know

what it is without knowing how to make it? That doesn't make any sense," I said.

"I dunno. Maybe the stodgy old warlocks who created it thought it looked cooler spelled that way. Anyway, the textbook said the Council banned the creation of it something like four hundred years ago and the formula has been lost ever since," Mallory said.

"Wow, so that's what Hilda meant when she said the right witch or warlock could extract ingredients from the Mean Green," I said — and why Lorelei told me about Sage's fascination with fire and her access to all of Hilda's things in the shop.

"Mean Green? What in Lilith's name are you talking about?" Mallory asked.

"Sorry, I'm several steps ahead of you here. I think I have an idea who might be our little firefly, but I don't have any clue how I'm going to get them to talk to me," I said.

"Who?"

"Sage Snow, Hilda's apprentice at Hypnotic Tonics," I said.

"Oh, I know her. Funny enough, she and I are working together on an Alchemy project at Veilside. I guess you'd know that if you hadn't gotten thrown out," Mallory said, and I sat bolt upright, ignoring her sarcasm.

"Wait, do you think you could arrange some sort of meeting with her for me? I mean, she seemed pretty eager to talk when I met her at Hypnotic Tonics the other day, but I don't think she'll be anywhere near as forthcoming with me if she's the one in the hot seat," I said.

"Yeah, I'm sure I could. The project is due in the next few days and we were supposed to get together soon to finish up our formula," Mallory said.

"Perfect. Can you text her now?" I asked, excited.

"Sure, give me a second," Mallory said as she dug for her phone in her robe's pockets, which were fit to burst. She whipped her phone out and a gaggle of other random items I didn't want to know about tumbled down her front. I watched in awe as her thumbs sped across the screen. She was a machine.

"Done. She's usually pretty fast about responding, so we'll see what she says. Hopefully, she isn't working at the shop today," Mallory said.

"Yeah, it wouldn't surprise me if they're open on Sundays," I said. Mallory held up a hand to silence me though as her eyes dashed across the message that'd just come across.

"Good news, she's free all day," Mallory said. "When should I ask her to meet and where?"

"As soon as possible and, uh, at Mooney's Diner?" I suggested.

Mallory looked at me sideways like it was the lamest idea she'd ever heard, but I couldn't think of anything better. Besides, three witches having lunch on a Sunday afternoon wouldn't look conspicuous.

I hadn't been to Mooney's since my first date with Beau, and the thought produced a pang in my heart. I still hadn't called him, despite my promise to Flora. I'd do it as soon as I could.

"Whatever, I guess it's fine," Mallory said and fired off a response. I sat chewing on my lips while we waited to hear back, but we didn't have to wait long.

"We're game," Mallory said. "Sage said she could meet me in the next forty-five minutes or so."

"Perfect. That'll give me time to sort through everything and catch you up so we're on the same page when we get there," I said.

"Sounds good," Mallory said as she typed to tell Sage it was a date.

When she was finished, I told her everything I'd learned so far: about all the trouble Hilda had been through getting her shop off the ground, how both Circe and Lorelei were involved in negotiations with the werewolves, and what Lorelei told me about how unusual Sage was — and about her apparent fixation on fire.

"This is going to be good," Mallory said as we hopped off the couch with only ten minutes left to get ourselves over to Mooney's.

"Wait, Sage doesn't know I'm coming, right?" I asked after I'd closed the door and locked it. If she did, she probably wouldn't have agreed to meet, but I had to be sure. I also didn't want to tip Sage off and give her time to prepare any answers.

"She's totally clueless," Mallory said. "Honestly, I almost feel sorry for the poor girl unleashing you on her like this."

"I won't be too much of an attack dog, I promise," I said.

"Please, you don't know how to be gentle when it comes to questioning people," Mallory said. "Don't they teach you that stuff in journalism school, or is that not really a thing in the non-magical world?"

"Trust me, there are more ethics classes than you would believe, but let's go," I said as I ushered her down the street.

We crossed town to Mooney's on the southside in record time, neither of us speaking much. All I could think about was the look sure to sprout on Sage's face when Mallory and I walked in together. I hoped she wouldn't run away screaming when she realized she'd been played.

At the entrance to the diner, Mallory stopped me.

"Are you sure you want to do this? I'm fine with going in there alone and scrapping the whole thing if you wanna bail," she said.

"No, it needs to happen. I'm curious what she'll say, especially now that I've got some background info on her. You go in first and warm her up, then shoot me a text when you're ready for me," I said.

"You got it," Mallory said and walked inside without another word. I hung around on the street and paced back and forth with my phone clutched in my hand while I waited to hear something from her. Passersby looked at me like I was plotting something nefarious, but I did my best to ignore them.

Finally, twenty minutes later, my phone vibrated. It was a simple message from Mallory that said "Ready." With a deep breath, I headed toward the diner and stepped into the assault of its retro interior and blaring music.

Thankfully, Mallory and Sage were seated in a booth toward the rear of the restaurant and Sage had her back turned. When Mallory caught sight of me, she spoke louder and faster like she was trying to cover up the sound of my footsteps but it only made Sage more suspicious.

I'd just reached the table when Sage turned to see what Mallory was looking at — and all the color drained from her freckled face.

"Oh, hi, Zoe. Funny we would run into each other here," Sage laughed, her septum piercing bouncing. She wore basic black robes with matching lipstick and her hair was pulled up into two messy pigtails.

"Yeah, sure is," I said as I made my way around and sat down in the booth next to Mallory. Sage furrowed her eyebrows.

"Are you two friends? I didn't know this was going to be a threesome," Sage said.

"We are. And it's not really a threesome so much as it's a one-on-one," I said, careful with my words.

"About what? I thought Mallory and I were going to work on our Alchemy project for school," Sage said.

"Yeah, you still can, but I have a few questions about Councilwoman Woods I want to ask you first," I said. Sage swallowed hard and drummed her fingers on the table, the numerous gaudy rings that adorned them click-clacking against the surface. Clearly, Circe was the last thing Sage wanted to talk about.

"You know what, I think I'll just catch up with you later when you're free, Mallory," Sage said and stood to leave.

"Unless you want to fail this project, I suggest you sit down and answer Zoe's questions," Mallory said. "I don't have any shame about intentionally screwing it up," she continued and a smile cracked my face. Mallory never ceased to surprise me.

"Fine," Sage said and collapsed back into the booth in a huff. "But

I don't know why you want to talk to me about her. I barely knew her."

"When I talked to you and Hilda at Hypnotic Tonics a couple days ago you mentioned that Lorelei Riddle had given you a lot of trouble," I said. Sage nodded.

"Yeah, I wasn't lying. You can ask anyone involved, they'll all tell you the same thing, but I don't know what that has to do with Circe," Sage said.

"I don't need to talk to anyone else. I asked Lorelei herself and she admitted it, more or less," I said. Sage raised her eyebrows at me.

"You did? Wow, I knew I liked you for a reason," Sage said, smiling.

"But that wasn't the only thing she told me about you," I said and her smile vanished. "I have reason to believe the fire that killed Councilwoman Woods was magical and I strongly suspect it was an alchemical formula that started it."

"Now you sound like Lorelei. Hilda told you our tonics are safe, and they are. But it's also true that a skilled witch or warlock could've easily pulled our creation apart for their own purposes," Sage said.

"True, but a shop assistant with access to all the materials and formulas that Hypnotic Tonics has in stock could've just as easily gone off and made something of their own," I said. Sage's face steeled.

"What? Are you seriously trying to say I'd put my career and my mentor's reputation on the line because I was upset about the way the Council treated us?" Sage asked. As a matter of fact, I wasn't going that direction at all just yet, but it was interesting to hear Sage come to that conclusion anyway.

"If the pointed hat fits," I said, shrugging. "Wild Fyre didn't just appear out of thin air to ignite Circe's house on its own, and you have access to more alchemical ingredients than anyone else besides Hilda in this town."

Sage squirmed in her seat, her face contorting as she worked through her anger.

"Wild Fyre?" she laughed. "Maybe you haven't put this together yet, super sleuth, but I'm still an apprentice, not some rogue mad scientist. Mallory knows how much I'm struggling in Alchemy at school anyway, so do you really think I could figure out how to make some sort of concoction like that?" Sage asked.

"She's not lying, she's absolutely abysmal at Alchemy. It's amazing to me that Hilda agreed to take her on as an apprentice,"

Mallory said and I had to bite back my laughter. Blunt should've been her middle name.

"Wow, thanks," Sage said, crossing her arms over her chest and staring out the frosted-glass window beside us.

"Hey, don't ask if you don't want to know," Mallory said.

"Even if you were the worst alchemist in the world, anyone can follow a formula that's already laid out for them. It's no different than following a recipe for baking," I said, watching Sage's face.

I didn't know whether or not Hilda actually had a formula for Wild Fyre, but if she did and Sage used it, I'd know from the look on her face — or find it in her thoughts if it came to that.

"Wild Fyre's illegal," Sage said.

"Thanks, Captain Obvious," Mallory muttered. "The stuff is so dangerous that it was banned hundreds of years ago, and yet, somebody clearly knows how to make it in this town," Mallory said.

It was a stretch to think someone who was allegedly awful at Alchemy could successfully make Wild Fyre, but Sage's ignorance could've been an act too. It wouldn't have been the first time I'd been led astray by a convincing actress.

"Look, even if I knew how to make Wild Fyre — and I don't — I was staying the night with Hilda at the shop when the fire broke out. Not even witches can get from one place to another that quickly. Besides, I wouldn't have been caught dead outside after the curfew went into effect," Sage said.

Wait, was she saying what I thought she was? The only citizens who weren't obligated to follow the curfew were werewolves and that was only because they couldn't control themselves under the Blood Moon.

Could it really have been a werewolf that went after Circe? If so, why? Was it a scorned member of the group negotiating with her for werewolf power and representation? It would make sense.

"But since you're digging, maybe you'd be interested to know about something I've seen," Sage said and my ears perked. "I don't know that it means anything. It could just be because of all the trouble we've been through, but it is weird."

"What are you talking about?" I asked.

"There's this vampire that's been hanging around the shop after dark taking pictures," Sage said, shivering. There was only one vampire photographer in all of Moon Grove that I knew of: Marcel Desfleurs at Grave Times. But why would he be out taking photos of Hypnotic Tonics in the dark?

"Why?" I asked.

"I don't know. I used to think it was because he knew about all the trouble we'd had with the Council and was trying to catch us doing something wrong to spin it into a story for his vampire gossip rag," Sage said.

"But you don't think that now?"

"I dunno what to think, but I wouldn't be surprised if we weren't the only ones he's been stalking. A vampire could move around under a curfew without being caught, especially if his powers were boosted by the Blood Moon like they say is possible," Sage said.

"Wait, even if he didn't have anything to do with Circe's death, if it's true he's been following people around at night it's also possible he caught something juicy on camera," Mallory said. I was already one step ahead of her.

"Yeah, like whoever lit Circe's house on fire," I said. "Looks like it's time to pay my competition a visit. Thanks for the tip, Sage."

"Sure, whatever. Are we done here?" she asked.

"Yup, I'll leave you two to it. Good luck with the project," I said with a wink and showed myself out of the diner to walk home.

On the way, I called Beau and didn't get an answer so I left a message asking if he'd like to have dinner the following night. Flora was right: the phone did work both ways, but it hadn't given me the comfort I wanted. Hopefully, he'd call me back soon.

To distract myself, I sent a text to Mallory:

>>*Me: Thanks for the help, I owe you big time.*

As usual, she wrote back right away:

>>*Mallory: You bet your broom you do, and I intend to collect.*

CHAPTER TEN

INSTEAD OF PUTTING the finishing touches on the small business story Mitch had assigned me the week before like I was supposed to be doing, I sat staring idly at my computer screen, unable to think about anything other than Marcel Desfleurs and Grave Times.

Finally, I gave up and went to talk to Mitch. As editor-in-chief of the Moon Grove Messenger, it was his responsibility to know everything about our competition — and I had a ton of questions.

I crossed the newsroom, careful not to have my head taken off by any of the various documents and office supplies soaring from desk to desk above me. Why couldn't Moon Grove just embrace email? It was far less dangerous.

Mitch's office door was closed so I knocked lightly.

"What is it? I'm busy," Mitch growled, his voice muffled.

"It's Zoe. Can we talk?" I asked and opened the door without waiting for an answer. Mitch was hunched over his keyboard hammering away at something. He looked up at me and sighed, his more-tangled-than-usual beard fluttering in his breath.

"You don't look so hot, boss. Blood Moon got you ill?" I asked as I closed the door behind me.

"Oh, stop, you're making me howl with laughter," Mitch said and rolled his eyes. "Aren't you supposed to be finishing a story for me? Deadline's in a few hours."

"I know, but I can't focus and this is somewhat relevant to the story," I said and took a seat across from him.

"Do I want to know?"

"It's Marcel Desfleurs. You know, the photographer over at Grave

Times," I said. Mitch bared his teeth at me and for a moment I worried he was going to go full wolf and tear me limb from limb.

"Yeah, I know who he is," he mumbled as he got a grip on himself. "What about him?"

"I think he might have some connection to Councilwoman Woods' death," I said. Mitch raised his eyebrows.

"Really? Why?"

"Well, I went to talk to Hilda Blackwood like you suggested a couple days ago and I met her assistant, Sage. Long story short, Sage was more interesting to me so I met with her again yesterday," I said.

"Yeah, and?"

"She said Marcel's been hanging around their shop after dark snapping pictures," I said.

"What? Why?"

"Yeah, that's exactly what I want to know," I laughed.

"I mean, as much as Grave Times says they're representing an 'unbiased view of life for vampires' in Moon Grove, everyone knows they only exist to publish rumors that make the witches look bad," Mitch said.

"To what end?" I asked.

"Good question. You'll have to ask Lucien Bellerose about that, but something tells me he's still salty about the Council's handling of vampire relations," Mitch said and my mouth dropped open.

Lucien was what many called the Undead Land Baron of Moon Grove — he owned or had a stake in nearly every piece of property in town. He also happened to be someone I'd interviewed previously in connection with a different murder.

"Wait, he owns Grave Times?" I asked.

"Are you kidding? What doesn't he own around here? That's why the paper's run out of his big office building over in the Vampire's Quarter."

"That changes things," I muttered. "So is that why you said Grave Times is going after witches in their coverage?"

"Absolutely, but I don't really know why Marcel would be interested in Hypnotic Tonics of all stories," Mitch said.

"Maybe for the same reason we are," I said. "I think he might know something, and Sage said she wouldn't be surprised if Marcel was following other people around too."

"Neither would I. He's vampire paparazzi so that's sort of his job," Mitch said.

"I think I should talk to him, and maybe Lucien too," I said. "You know, use the same excuse about covering small businesses. They'll eat it up."

"Please, Lucien's way too savvy for that. Besides, that story's due by close of business today, remember?" Mitch asked, eyeing me. "So maybe you should be back at your desk finishing that instead of bothering me."

"It was nice talking to you too," I said and stuck my tongue out at him as I stood. He smirked. "What are you working on anyway? I've never seen you type so fast."

"Nothing," Mitch said and smashed the buttons on his keyboard to lock his screen when I leaned over to peek at it.

"Don't make me jump inside your brain to find out," I said.

"Don't make me assign you to write puff pieces for the rest of the month," Mitch said.

"Touché," I said and made to leave. Mitch sighed.

"Since I know you're gonna go to Grave Times no matter what I say, at least promise me you won't make us look bad," Mitch said. I stopped and turned to face him again.

"I'm an expert at ruining reputations, including my own, so you've got nothing to worry about!" I said and left him to chew on it like a dog with a bone.

☾

BELLEROSE ENTERPRISES' exterior looked no less intimidating than it had the first time I'd been. The thick glass front doors, tinted black as ink to block out any and all sun during the day — it was a vampire's place of business, after all — cast the moon's blinding reflection back at me.

The only thing that'd changed was the small addition of "Grave Times" to the sign posted out front.

My palms sweaty, I reached for the door handle and pulled. It took more effort than I remembered, but maybe Lucien had upgraded the glass to heavier, sturdier material. Lilith knew he had the money for it.

The narrow hallway lined on either side by uncomfortable metal chairs led to another wall of glass — and to my dismay, the same vampire secretary sitting behind it.

Céline glanced up from filing her nails, her eyes peeking over the top of her horn-rimmed glasses. She smirked, her hot red lipstick like a slash of fresh blood across her face. It gave me the creeps.

"Bonsoir, Ms. Clarke," she said. "I must say, I'm surprised to see you again."

"What can I say, I'm the gift that keeps on giving," I said and

Céline's smirk widened into a smile. As rude as she was to me the last time I'd come, I'd grown on her.

"I'm sorry to disappoint you, but Monsieur Bellerose isn't in this evening," she said.

"That's okay, I'm actually here to talk to Marcel Desfleurs," I said. Céline raised her eyebrows.

"I see. Let me page him," she said and reached for the phone on her desk. They spoke for a few seconds and then, in a blur of motion, Céline stood beside me on the other side of the glass, her emptied chair spinning.

"This way," Céline said, gesturing at the only door leading through the glass, which I hadn't realized was open until now. I would never get used to the super speed of vampires.

"Thanks," I muttered and went through. Céline's pumps clicked across the tile behind me as we walked another hall perforated by dozens more doors on either side. I knew from experience that Lucien's decadent office was at the very end, marked by a set of overindulgent carved double doors, but we never made it that far.

Céline stopped me halfway down the hall. An unimpressive plaque that read "Grave Times" hung outside the door. Céline tugged the badge she wore on a retractable necklace and held it to the security pad. The lock clicked open and she pushed the door for me.

Marcel sat just inside on the edge of one of the dozen or so desks that lined the floor in neat rows. Other than the lack of flying objects and staff other than Marcel, the newsroom at Grave Times didn't look much different from the Messenger's.

"Good evening, Zoe," Marcel said, smiling. "I'll take it from here, Céline. Merci."

"Avec plaisir," Céline said and disappeared, the door softly clicking closed on its own.

"You know, I've been wondering when you'd pay us a visit," Marcel said.

"Why's that?" I asked, instantly cautious, my shoulders creeping up toward my ears.

"I'm a journalist, you're a journalist, it just sort of makes sense," he said.

"I dunno if I'd call what you do journalism, so I guess we'll have to agree to disagree," I said. Marcel chuckled. He pushed off the desk and flicked his black curls out of his face.

"If only more people these days knew how to do that," he said. "Anyway, what can I help you with? I assume you have questions."

"I've heard you've been scoping out Hypnotic Tonics," I said. "Why?"

"They're interesting," Marcel said, smirking as he tucked his hands in the pocket of his jeans. What kind of vampire wore jeans anyway?

"Agreed, but that didn't answer my question," I said. "What's so interesting about them?"

"They're selling what effectively amounts to controlled substances," Marcel said. "In a normal world, the Council never would've allowed a shop like that to exist. But nothing's been normal in this town for months."

I could vouch for that.

"Fair enough, but why take pictures of them after dark? I mean, aside from the whole not being able to be outside during the day thing," I said. Marcel shrugged.

"Even if I could work during the day, I've seen enough in my time to know that people are much more forthcoming in the dark," he said.

"Yeah, I guess that sorta comes with the territory of snooping on people, doesn't it?" I asked. Marcel shook his head, his curls swinging.

"Some call it snooping, I call it intelligence gathering," Marcel said. "The thing is, people are so much more honest with my cameras than they are with me."

"Probably because they don't know they're being photographed," I said.

"Yes, probably," Marcel agreed, smiling.

"Where were you the night Circe Woods' house burned?" I asked, my patience running thin.

"Wow, what a segue," Marcel laughed. "But to answer your question, I was here sorting through my latest round of photos," Marcel said.

"Photos of what?" I asked.

"Photos of whom," he corrected. "But you already know the answer to that."

"Hilda?"

"Yes, among others," Marcel said. Others? What — or whom, to use his words — did he mean?

"Why were you taking photos of Hilda and whoever else that night?"

"I've been following them since Hypnotic Tonics opened and went undetected until I forgot to turn off the flash on my camera and Hilda's assistant noticed," Marcel said.

"How professional," I said, and Marcel chuckled.

"Even after hundreds of years behind the camera, I still make mistakes from time to time. Stake me," he said. "Anyway, I had a feeling something wasn't quite right with that shop and it turns out my suspicions were correct."

"How so?"

"They have an interesting business arrangement, that's for sure," Marcel said. "It's odd to see werewolves making pit stops there in the middle of the night."

"What are you talking about?"

"It would be easier for me just to show you. I mean, assuming you really want to know," Marcel said.

My mind raced. Of course I did, but I had no idea what I was about to learn — or if I could trust Marcel's photos in the first place. Between the magic of Moon Grove and the magic of Photoshop, who was to say his photos weren't altered? Grave Times did have a reputation for publishing false stories.

"Your silence speaks volumes. Wait here," Marcel said and disappeared into the newsroom in a whirl of motion and color. Seconds later, he popped back into existence beside me with a handful of photo prints.

He passed me the stack and my heart thrummed as I saw the date stamp in the bottom right corner of the first photo: the same day of the fire. But I couldn't make out anything in the picture, it just seemed black with a spattering of stars.

"I don't see anything," I said.

"Keep going through them, you will," Marcel said. I flipped to the next photo and despite the darkness, I made out the unmistakable façade of Hypnotic Tonics thanks mostly to the illuminated tonic vending machine outside.

The following frame showed the shop lit up inside and the shadow of someone or something in the main window. In the next, Marcel had zoomed in on a gap in the curtains and captured what could only be Hilda with her untamed hair.

"There's more," Marcel said. "You haven't gotten to the best part yet. I changed lenses and must've hit the wrong button in the process because this is around the time my flash went off."

The next picture was more or less the same as the last, so I breezed past it for another — and my heart fell into my stomach. The curtains were flung open and Sage was in the window, scowling. Behind her, a bald man covered in tattoos stood with his face twisted in rage, an empty vial in one hand, a wad of cash in the other.

It was Tony Romano, the same werewolf who'd been escorted out of the Council meeting when they announced the Blood Moon curfew.

"Is that...?"

"Tony Romano? Yes, it is," Marcel said. I dropped the rest of the photos on the nearest desk, feeling weightless and unable to look at any more.

"What were they doing?"

"I don't know, but it sure looks like some sort deal was taking place," Marcel said. "And if they were selling tonics on the sly to Tony, who else were they selling to without approval?"

The image of the stopper I'd found near Circe's house burned in my mind. Between it, the Blood Moon, Marcel's photos, and the curfew exemption, it didn't paint a pretty picture for the werewolves. There was no way Marcel's photos were doctored — the looks on the faces of Sage and Tony both told me that.

So was it Tony who'd killed Circe? He had the right motive.

"Why didn't you turn these photos into the police?" I breathed.

"Are you hearing yourself? The police are all werewolves, Zoe. They'd bury the story as quickly as they'd like to bury us vampires," Marcel said.

He was right, but it only made me feel worse.

"Are you going to publish these then?" I asked. Marcel smiled.

"That depends on what your plans are," he said. "We could work together, the Times and the Messenger. We could figure this out."

"Why? What's in it for you?"

"I'm a journalist, Zoe, I live for the pursuit of truth," Marcel said. I didn't believe him for a second, but he knew things I didn't and there was no denying how useful his skills might be.

"Okay, but I'm calling the shots," I said and Marcel beamed.

"I assumed," he said.

"Good. What do you know about Tony?"

"Not much. He owns a pizza joint in the Werewolves' Quarter called Pupperoni Pizza," Marcel said and I had to fight back my laughter.

"Clever," I coughed.

"I thought so too," he said. "What do you say we meet there tomorrow night around six and hit him with a double whammy? You go in for the interview and I'll hang back to get photo proof in case he tries anything funny."

"Deal," I said and we shook on it but I couldn't help wondering if I'd made a deal with the devil.

CHAPTER ELEVEN

I WAS JUST WALKING out of the Messenger's office the following afternoon when my phone rang in my bag. My heart skipped a beat when I saw Beau's name on the screen — maybe he wasn't angry with me after all.

"Hey, I'm so glad to hear from you," I answered, beaming. Beau chuckled and tingles ran down my spine.

"Sorry it took me so long to get back to you," he said, exasperated. "It's been a crazy couple of weeks at Channel 666 between the Blood Moon and houses burning down."

"It's okay, I understand. I've been stretched thin myself," I said.

"I can imagine, you poor thing. Hey, I know I'm a day late, but does that offer for dinner together still stand?" Beau asked.

"Of course," I said, thrilled. "I was starting to think you weren't ever going to talk to me again, so that's a relief."

"What? Why?"

"Come on, you know why. I made a fool of myself in front of the entire town and dragged you into it too," I said.

"Oh, griffin's feathers," Beau dismissed me. "When are you gonna stop piling on yourself about that?"

"Probably never," I said and Beau laughed.

"Well I know what'll take your mind off it, at least for a little while," he said.

"Oh yeah? What's that?"

"Sharing a nice hot pizza with one of the best-looking guys in all of Moon Grove," Beau said and a lightbulb went off in my head.

"That sounds perfect. I know just the place," I said.

"You do?"

"Yeah. Have you heard anything about a restaurant called Pupperoni Pizza?" I asked.

"I have, but they weren't good. Why do I get the feeling you're buttering me up for something?"

"Guilty as charged," I said.

"Who are we interrogating this time?" Beau sighed.

"Wow, reading me like a book," I laughed. "Honestly, maybe no one at all."

"Why not?"

"I don't know if they're going to be there or if they'll talk to me," I said.

"Who?"

"The owner, Tony Romano."

"You mean the werewolf that got escorted out of the Council meeting for throwing a fit about the curfew?" Beau asked.

"Yup, that's the one."

"Great. What could possibly go wrong?" he asked.

"So I take it that means we have a date?"

"I could never say no to you, even if it means putting my life in danger," Beau said and my face flushed. "Can I swing by your place around six?" That left me less than half an hour to get home and ready, but I wasn't about to lose my chance.

"I'll be waiting," I said.

"Good. See you soon," Beau said and hung up.

I dropped my phone back into my bag with butterflies in my stomach and dashed toward home, still stunned Beau wasn't afraid to be seen in public with me after my little stunt. We'd been dating for less than a month and I couldn't believe how well we fit together after such a short time. Maybe it wasn't an accident that he was the first person I ever met in Moon Grove.

When I opened the front door, Flora was already in the kitchen cooking something or another. Luna sat on the couch licking one of her paws but froze when I came inside.

"Fancy meeting you here," she said.

"Hilarious," I said, kicking the door closed behind me. I tossed my bag on the couch as I hurried to my room to clean up and change before Beau arrived.

"What's the hurry? You got a hot date tonight or something?" Luna asked, trotting along behind me.

"As a matter of fact, I do," I said.

"Meeeeeeow," Luna said and I swore I saw a smile on her little kitty face.

"Oh, stop. It's not nearly as salacious as you make it sound," I said.

"Zoe, is that you?" Flora called from the kitchen.

"Yeah," I shouted back.

"Are you hungry? I'm making spaghetti," Flora said.

"I'd love to join you but I'm going out with Beau for dinner," I said. Seconds passed without a reply and then Flora's face appeared in my doorway.

"So I take it that means you finally called him?" she asked, smiling.

"Yeah. It took a few days for him to get back to me but he did," I said.

"Good, I'm glad to hear it. Where are you two going?"

"Pupperoni Pizza," I said, and Flora furrowed her eyebrows.

"Really? Why?"

"Reasons," I said, looking away from her. Flora sighed and shook her head.

"Even if I didn't have a built-in lie detector, I can always tell you're lying when you use that excuse," Flora said.

"Fine, I'm going to talk to the owner of the place," I said.

"For what?"

"I don't have time to explain. Beau's gonna be here any minute to pick me up and I still haven't even washed my face," I said.

"Oh, okay, sorry to interrupt," Flora said and disappeared back into the kitchen.

"That just leaves more spaghetti for me," Luna said, licking her chops.

"Since when do you eat spaghetti? You're definitely the weirdest cat I've ever met in my life," I said.

"Or am I?"

"Go back to cleaning yourself, I've got my own cleaning to do," I said.

"I bet I'll do a better job of it," Luna said as she left, her tail swishing around the corner. I flew into the adjacent bathroom and wet my hair and face in the sink. Though I wanted to wash both, I only had time for one — and my face was much more important, so I scrubbed it with a bar of soap.

With my face clean and my red curls tied up in a towel, I went back into the bedroom and threw on the best t-shirt and jeans I could find because mixing robes with pizza was a grease stain waiting to happen.

I'd just stepped out into the living room when the doorbell rang.

Beau was nothing if not punctual. Luna had returned to licking herself on the couch beside my bag.

"Meeeeeeow," she called after me as I went to answer the door and I scratched her head to shush her before scooping up my bag. I flung the door open and melted when I saw Beau on the other side dressed in a casual pink polo and jeans, his chestnut hair slicked back.

"Hey, you ready to go?" Beau asked, flashing me his perfect smile.

"Definitely," I said. He offered me his arm and I slipped mine through it.

"Be home before eleven, missy! And stay out of trouble!" Luna said from the couch but I ignored her and closed the door.

"She's awfully strict," Beau said and I laughed.

"Yeah, she sure is," I agreed and the conversation tapered as we walked down Swiftsage toward Crescent Street. I hoped he knew where we were going because I didn't have a clue.

"How's your grandma doing?" Beau asked when we rounded the corner and headed south.

"Amazingly well, all things considered," I said. Beau smiled.

"She's a firecracker, isn't she? Now I know where you get your personality and grit from," he said.

"Yes, among other, less desirable traits."

"They're all part of the bigger picture, which I love," Beau said, his smile widening. I thought I might ignite. "Anyway, are you gonna tell me why you want to talk to the unpredictable owner of a werewolf pizza joint before we get there?"

"It's a long story, but the shortened version is I think he might've had something to do with Circe's house burning down," I said. Beau came to a sudden halt, jerking me back with him.

"You do? Why?"

"I saw some, erm, questionable photos of him last night," I said.

"I'm not sure I want to know but I'm going to ask anyway: what sort of questionable photos and where did you see them?"

"He was at Hypnotic Tonics after hours, and I saw the photos when I went to speak to Marcel Desfleurs last night," I said. Beau shook his head.

"I knew introducing you two was trouble waiting to happen," he said. "Is there anything else I should know about this?"

"Well, actually…"

"Spill it, Zoe," Beau said.

"Marcel's coming too," I said and Beau sighed.

"For what? I thought we were on a date."

"We are. I already had plans to meet Marcel at Pupperoni tonight, but I hadn't seen you in a while so I wasn't going to say no when you asked to have dinner together. I thought I'd fly two witches with one broom," I said.

"I don't understand. Why is Marcel coming?"

"To do what he does best: take pictures," I said.

"Of Tony?"

"Yeah, and who or whatever else might be interesting," I said.

"You never stop working, do you?"

"Not when there's an active murder case to be solved," I said, shrugging. "But don't worry, there's a good chance Tony won't even talk to me and no one will know Marcel is there, for obvious reasons."

"I don't like this," Beau said. "We're gonna be in the heart of the Werewolves' Quarter of town, and they're gonna look at us funny."

"Why would they—oh, yeah, the whole werewolves hating shifters thing," I said. "What is that? You'll have to explain that to me someday."

"There's that, but also because the two of us are well-known reporters, for better or worse," he said. "We aren't exactly incognito is all I'm saying."

"I'm not trying to be," I said. "That's where Marcel comes into play. Be cool, we'll just share a pizza like we were on a normal date and everything will be fine."

"That's what you always say but then you go running off in the middle of dinner," Beau said. A fight with him was the last thing on Earth I wanted, so I bit my tongue.

"That won't happen this time, I promise," I said and linked my fingers between his. "We're just gathering some intel, you know, observing. Besides, I could use an extra pair of eyes to help — and a supercharged nose like yours."

Though I could tell he wasn't happy, eventually Beau sighed and shrugged.

"All right, I guess it's not the weirdest thing you've asked me to help you with since we met," he said and I laughed.

"Thank you," I said and pecked a kiss on his cheek. Beau flushed and chewed his lip.

"Let's get this over," he said and started walking. It occurred to me I'd never set foot in Moon Grove's Werewolves' Quarter — I hadn't had any reason to until now — and I had no idea what to expect.

But when we turned left and walked along a road named Fang

Street, I realized there wasn't anything that could've prepared me for the experience anyway.

Halfway down, the small brick buildings and iron street lamps that characterized most of Moon Grove gave way to darkness and run-down wooden houses, many with boarded-up windows and doors. Were they meant to keep intruders out — or to keep wild werewolves inside?

A chill ran down my spine at the thought.

"Are you okay?" Beau asked though he didn't sound all that okay himself.

"Y-yeah, just taking it all in," I mumbled, staring at the wooden wall of the nearest house scarred by four distinct slashes I could only assume came from claws. "I had no idea the werewolves lived so…" I trailed, casting for the word.

"Modestly? Well, turning into a wild animal once a month makes it hard to keep a job, even in a paranormal town like this," Beau whispered. "But don't dare let any of them hear you talk like that."

"Got it," I said as we continued down the street.

Oddly enough, not a soul passed as we walked, not even when we came to a dimly-lit village circle lined with shops and restaurants. They were all empty. A flashing neon sign with several burnt out letters attached to a dingy, sketchy looking building caught my eye: "Pupperni Pzza" it read.

Modest, indeed.

"That's it," Beau said, nodding at the sign to confirm what I feared.

"Charming," I said.

"Oh, just wait. It's positively cozy inside," Beau said and led me toward the restaurant. I hoped Marcel was out in the darkness somewhere watching us in case we didn't come out again.

The smell of baking dough and marinara sauce invaded my nose as we approached and I had to admit it smelled delicious — though I wouldn't have dreamed of eating anything in the place.

A rotted wooden door swung precariously from rusted hinges as Beau pushed it open. Inside, a woman in a leopard print spaghetti-strap shirt sat at one of the half dozen card tables admiring her French-manicured nails. I couldn't take my eyes off them; they had to be at least four inches long.

She jumped when she saw us but came over in a hurry, her too-tall heels clicking across the tile in time with the bouncing of her black and bleach-blonde curls against her shoulders.

"Hey, welcome to Pupperoni. I'm Adriana, your hostess," she

said in a thick New Jersey accent and I had to contain my laughter. She looked like a walking stereotype.

"Is it just the two of ya?" Adriana asked and Beau nodded. Adriana clawed two menus out of a holster built into the wall and gestured for us to follow her.

A man in chef's garb stood behind a glass display case showing off various types of pizza, all of them drab and stale. His back was turned as he shoved a wooden pizza tray into a giant coal-fired oven. A tall white hat covered his head but I still couldn't have mistaken him for anyone other than Tony Romano.

As if he'd sniffed us walking in — and he probably had — Tony spun around with his nose wrinkled and his clothes covered in flour.

"I knew I smelled something rotten," Tony said. He dusted his hands off on his shirt and crossed his arms over his chest, revealing several more tattoos on each.

"Oh my Gawd, Tony, watch ya mouth," Adriana said, scowling at him.

"Mind your business, Adriana. What are you doing here, halfie?" Tony asked and Adriana gasped, clapping a clawed hand over her mouth. More gold than I'd ever seen in one place flashed on her fingers.

Beau flushed and stared at the floor. Halfie? Was that some sort of insult to shifters?

"Nothing," Beau snapped. "I just came to share some of your world-class hospitality and pizza with my girlfriend."

"Please, ignore him, doll. We're all fahmily here so make yahselves at home," Adriana said, waving us forward.

She selected one of the rickety tables by the back and Beau pulled a folding chair out from under it for me. A plastic tablecloth in a red-and-white checkerboard design draped into my lap when I sat. Classy.

Tony tossed his hat down on the counter as he stepped out around it, lumbering toward our table with a scowl.

"I said, what are you doing here, *halfie*?" Tony growled, leaning over us. He reeked of stale smoke and alcohol and bags bigger than the one on my shoulder hung from his eyes. No wonder he had a temper. If I looked as rugged as he did, I'd be grouchy too.

All of Beau's confidence seemed to have run out of his ears, so I cleared my throat.

"I've heard great things about your deep dish, so I think we'd like to order a large with pepperoni, sausage, and extra cheese, please," I said. Tony glared at me, his nostrils flaring, clearly not amused.

"Order it somewhere else," Tony said.

"Antonio Gabriel Romano!" Adriana snapper. "We haven't had a customuh all day, mind ya manners," she scolded him.

"Then you serve them," Tony barked and stormed off through a side door into what appeared to be his office. It was barely bigger than a broom closet from what I could see — though there was a tiny, uncovered window built into the wall. Hopefully, Marcel knew where to look.

Smoke curled over Tony's shoulder as he fired up a cigar and shook out the match. That explained the stench on his clothes.

"Oh my Gawd, I'm so sorry," Adriana said.

"It's okay. We should go," Beau said.

"No way. I didn't come all the way here for nothing," I hissed as I reached for Beau's hand.

"Please, stay. Tony's just got a hair in his pizza today because business is slow," Adriana said. "Ignore him."

"All right," Beau sighed and sat down. Phew, crisis averted.

"Excuse me, Adriana, do you have a restroom I could use?" I asked.

"Sure, doll, it's right ova there," Adriana said, pointing one of her talons toward another door at the back of the restaurant. "Can I get ya somethin' to drink in the meantoime?"

"Two waters, please," I said, though I had no intention of drinking mine.

"You got it," she said and clicked away behind the counter toward the humming drink machine, her long legs swishing in her jean skirt. I pushed back from the table and acted like I was going to the bathroom — but took a hard right into Tony's office instead. Beau hissed at me to stop but I paid him no mind.

Tony sat with his back to me at a lopsided desk lined by stacks of cash held together by rubber bands. My eyes went wide at the sight and it took me a few seconds to get my voice back as I watched him counting several hundred notes.

His restaurant was as dead as my investigation, so where — and how — had he gotten all this money?

"That's an awful lot of money you've got there, Mr. Romano," I said. Tony jolted in his chair and whirled around, his cigar bouncing between his lips and shaking ashes into his lap. He tried to block my view of the money but it was too late.

"Whaddaya think you're doin' in here?!" he shouted, jumping up from the chair wild-eyed.

"Sorry, I guess I took the wrong door to the bathroom," I said. I wasn't about to let him intimidate me. I'd faced far scarier.

"Sure ya did. Why are you here, Ms. Clarke?" Tony snapped. When I didn't reply, he laughed and shook his head.

"You think I didn't recognize you sitting with the halfie? I know all about you. Just another hotshot reporter making life difficult for everybody else trying to make an honest living," Tony said.

"You call this honest?" I asked, nodding at the money. Tony scoffed.

"I'm a made man. I don't have anything to hide."

"Okay. Then where were you the night Circe Woods' house burned to the ground?" I asked, hoping to catch him in a lie.

"Right here, wasn't I, Adriana?" Tony asked, jabbing his cigar through the air over my shoulder. I turned to find Adriana standing with her hands on her hips and her bottom lip between her teeth. She shrugged.

"Yeah, sure, of course ya was," Adriana said. "Where else would ya have been?"

"So there you go," Tony said and popped his cigar back into his mouth to take a long drag.

"Then why have I seen photos of you inside Hypnotic Tonics after hours that night?" I asked. Tony's mouth fell open, threatening to send his cigar tumbling to the ground, but he caught himself.

"Zoe, what are you—" Beau hissed from the table, but Tony raised a hand to silence him.

"Wait a second, you *what*?"

"You heard me," I said, looking him straight in the eye. I didn't think I could read a werewolf's mind, but I wasn't above giving it the good ol' college try.

"I dunno what you're talking about."

"You're lying. I've seen the pictures. Why were you at Hypnotic Tonics after hours the night Circe Woods died?" I asked.

"All right, fine. Not that it's any of your business, but Hilda and I have a lil' agreement," Tony said, avoiding my eyes and drawing circles of smoke with his cigar as he waved it.

"Which is?"

"The Council's been givin' them a hard time about their shop and products and whatnot, so they agreed to pay me in exchange for getting the Council off their backs," Tony said.

"You mean because you were negotiating with Circe and Lorelei Riddle so you had some sway?" I asked.

"You know about that too, huh? Doesn't matter. Yeah, I had some weight to throw around. If the Council wouldn't agree to ease off Hypnotic Tonics, I'd stir up some trouble for them politically with the werewolves," Tony said.

"And you got free tonics in exchange so it was a win-win," I said. Namely, Mean Greens.

"You scratch my back, I'll scratch yours," Tony said. I tried not to think about that image too much. Tony was hairy even by werewolf standards.

"Right. But why did you keep going to Hypnotic Tonics after the shop was allowed to open?" I asked. "They don't seem to need your protection anymore."

"They owe me money," Tony said and my eyebrows raised.

"For what?"

"I gave Hilda a loan to start her shop. You didn't really think a batty old witch like her came up with the cash on her own did you?" Tony asked.

I hadn't thought about it, but it made perfect sense. Hilda was asleep the first time I'd gone into Hypnotic Tonics so she didn't strike me as being particularly ambitious. But then again, I still hadn't figured out where Tony got all his money.

"How much does she owe you?"

"More than she'll ever make at that hocus pocus shop," Tony said. "But that's why I keep coming by, to make sure she pays me one way or another."

"Even if it's in the form of tonics?" I asked and Tony scowled.

"That's none of your business," he said.

"It is if one of them made you go AWOL and kill a Councilwoman — it would clear your path to power and scare your 'client' into paying up," I said.

"That's crazy, listen to yourself. Look, I know things around here might seem a lil' sketchy, but I swear I'm not up to anything," Tony said.

Sketchy didn't even scratch the surface. Between Tony's lies and the thousands of bills stacked in his office, I found it hard to believe he had nothing at all to hide — but whatever crimes he'd committed, I didn't think he'd killed Circe. It would've drawn too much attention to his other, erm, enterprises — which was probably why he was so annoyed with me digging.

"But I tell you what, I wouldn't put it past Hilda to do something like that. Who knows what she's putting in those potions of hers. I swear it's killing her brain cells, and I'm sure I'm not the only one she owes money to," Tony said.

Could Hilda really have taken one of her own concoctions and gone postal on Circe? She didn't seem like the type to hurt anyone, not even a fly, but I'd learned the hard way looks could be deceiving. Besides, Hilda wasn't any less likely a candidate than Tony.

I needed to find out who else Hilda owed money to — and why. It could've been the key to everything; follow the money, as the saying goes.

"Zoe, maybe we should get going," Beau said, clutching my hand in his and squeezing it desperately. I hadn't realized he was there. Still, I'd gotten as much as I probably could out of Tony, so I gave in to Beau's pleas.

"Sorry to have bothered you, Mr. Romano," I said.

"Psh, please. Something tells me it won't be the last time I hear from you," he said as he flicked the ashes off the tip of his cigar onto the floor. Thank Lilith I hadn't eaten anything made there.

"We'll show ourselves out," Beau said, dragging me by the hand out of Tony's office.

"Oh, come on, you aren't even gonna eat something?" Adriana asked.

"Maybe next time," Beau said with a perfect fake smile.

"See you around, halfie," Tony said, smiling back. Beau's face flushed and he walked me out of the restaurant and back down Fang Street in a hurry. When we were far enough away I was sure no one would overhear, I stopped him.

"What's the whole 'halfie' thing about?" I asked. Beau sighed and shook his head.

"Like I said, werewolves don't like shifters," he said.

"Right, but why? I don't understand. Aren't you part of the same family?"

"Technically, yes, but the werewolves look down on us. While no one knows for sure, the story goes that shifters didn't exist until werewolves started mingling with humans if you know what I mean," Beau said.

"So they hate you because they think you diluted the family tree? That's ridiculous," I said.

"I know. Not many people — werewolves or shifters — believe it, but there are still a few traditionalists hanging around like Tony," Beau said.

"Wait, is that why you and Mitch don't get along?"

"No, no. He's nothing like Tony in that regard. Mitch and I had girl problems years ago, but it doesn't matter now," Beau said.

"Okay, it's probably better I don't know then. Anyway, did you see all the money Tony had? What the heck has he been up to to get that?" I asked, changing the subject.

"No idea, but I bet it wasn't legal," Beau said.

"Definitely not," I said. "Do you think he could be in the mafia or something? I mean, he owns a pizza parlor..."

"A werewolf mafia run out of a pizza parlor? Like Pizzagate? Seriously, Zoe?"

"Hey, he had thousands of bills in there. Besides, it's Moon Grove. Anything's possible," I said with a shrug. "I just hope Marcel got some shots of it all from outside."

"Speaking of, how do you even know he's here?" Beau asked, squinting into the darkness like he had any hope of spotting a vampire after dark anyway.

"I don't," I said, but something told me Marcel wouldn't miss out on an opportunity like this.

"So now what?" Beau asked. "That wasn't much of a date."

"Sorry, I'll make it up to you — and no more surprises, I promise. Wanna go grab a coffee or a MagiShake or something?" I asked.

"I'd love to," Beau said and offered me his arm again. I took it and as we walked I glanced over my shoulder one last time — and could've sworn I saw the blur of a vampire dashing through the woods away from the restaurant.

It put a smile on my face. I couldn't wait to see what Marcel captured.

CHAPTER TWELVE

INSTEAD OF PRETENDING to work and failing, I spent most of the afternoon waiting to hear from Marcel — and researching the werewolves.

Luckily for me, the Moon Grove Historical Society had digitized the Parapages years ago and made them available free online. There was tons of information about the history and lore of the werewolves generally, along with the role they'd played in Moon Grove's collective story.

As I'd already learned, the Council decided hundreds of years ago to open up the borders to any sort of paranormal being, not just witches or warlocks, in order for the town to survive. But interestingly enough, the werewolves were one of the last groups to be permitted inside.

The rest of their history, however, was even less rosy. Until recently, not even the paranormal groups in Moon Grove knew how to handle or manage the transformation of werewolves during the full moon, which led to them being segregated in their own part of town where no one else dared go, even when there wasn't any risk — and that was to say nothing of a Blood Moon.

But considering how often those happened, and how often the town would have to deal with their effects, it stunned me to learn the Council hadn't come up with a better solution than a curfew. Suspiciously, the article didn't detail what effects the Blood Moon had on werewolves. But if the official historical record of Moon Grove didn't have the answer, who did?

I sighed and pushed back from my computer to rub my eyes. I'd done a lot of investigating but come up with precious few leads. As far as I could find, there was nothing about a Blood Moon that would make a werewolf want to set a house on fire — much less deliberately target the home of a prominent witch like Circe.

So it couldn't have been a random attack. The more likely answer was that whoever had torched Circe's house was someone who knew her or otherwise had a connection to her. There were a lot of moving pieces, but they didn't fit together in any way that made sense.

First, there was no arguing the vial stopper I'd found outside Circe's house was connected to Hypnotic Tonics. It led to Hilda, the shop's owner, who seemed more than a little odd to say the least, and her assistant, Sage, clearly had a chip on her shoulder about the treatment they'd gotten from Lorelei Riddle and the rest of the Council.

But the only link I'd found between Hypnotic Tonics and the Council was Tony Romano, werewolf and pizza parlor owner who'd evidently given a loan to Hilda to start her shop and was involved in political negotiations with Circe on behalf of the werewolves.

But why was Tony Romano of all people chosen to speak for the werewolves? He seemed like he had an uncontrollable temper, to say the least, so how could he negotiate anything without breaking people's faces when he didn't get his way?

I couldn't shake the feeling I was missing something, but no matter how I turned the info over in my head, I couldn't make the pieces fit together. Tony suspected that Hilda owed other people money too, which in and of itself was worth investigating. But it wasn't likely Hilda would give me access to her financial reports, so how else could I find out?

My cell phone rang on the desk beside me and my brow furrowed when I saw it was Raina. The only reason she'd be calling in the middle of the day was if it related to Grandma. Panicked, I snatched the phone off the desk and smashed the button to accept the call.

"Hello?" I asked.

"Zoe, Sugar, it's Grandma," Grandma Elle's drawl came through and I breathed a sigh of relief. If she had the wits to call me, whatever she had to say probably wasn't urgent.

"Hey, Gram. What's going on? I'm at work, I can't talk long," I said.

"I know, I'm sorry to bother you in the middle of the day like this. Listen, I've been workin' through some stuff with Raina since I been here and I think we need to talk," Grandma said. The relief I'd felt before fell out of my mouth like my spirit had been ejected.

"That sounds serious," I said.

"Now don't you go gettin' your panties in a wad, it ain't worth losin' your cool over," Grandma said. "But anyway, it probably ain't a good idea to be talkin' about it over the phone, so do you think you could come over here after work tonight?"

"Yeah, definitely, I don't have any other plans," I said — and even if I did, I would've canceled them for this. My hands were so slick with sweat I worried I might drop the phone.

"Okay, good, good. When are ya done over there?" Grandma asked.

"Punch out time is at five, but I'm sure I can leave a little earlier if you need me to," I said. I glanced at the clock and my heart sank when I realized it was only three o'clock. Waiting for five to roll around would be torture.

"No, ain't no need for that. I don't need you gettin' yerself in trouble on account of me again. Just come over when you're finished," Grandma said.

"All right. How are things over there? Are you alone?" I asked.

"Not, I got Tierney here in my lap, as always," Grandma said. "Raina's at work, obviously, but she set me up with some crocheting needles and thread so I got more than enough to occupy my time."

I wished I could say the same. At least Grandma's revelation would give me something to think about other than Circe and whoever might've killed her.

"Okay, good. You need me to bring anything when I come? Any food or anything?"

"No, we're good. I'll see ya in a couple hours, Sugar," Grandma said.

"All right. Love you," I said.

"Love you too," Grandma said and hung up.

I sat staring at the phone in my hand unable to process what happened. For all I knew, Grandma could just be waiting to tell me she was going home and that Raina had figured out a way to make that happen — but there was something in the back of my brain telling me otherwise.

Thankfully, my computer dinged with an p-mail alert and pulled me out of my negative spiral. I switched over to my p-mail app and gasped when I saw I had a message from Marcel. I had no idea how he got my work address, but I wasn't complaining.

With my heart racing, I clicked into the message and a smile the likes of which I hadn't worn in months cracked my face when dozens of photos loaded. There were a few of Beau and I walking into Pupperoni Pizza, but the majority of them were shot from outside the restaurant looking through the small window into Tony's office.

And there was no missing the stacks of cash inside, rendered in beautiful high definition. I wasn't sure what if anything I could do with the photos, but it reassured me to have them nonetheless. Marcel had made good on his end of the bargain. Maybe he wasn't so untrustworthy after all.

I clicked to send a reply:

>>*Me: Excellent work! Anything interesting pop out at you? I got a lot of dirt talking to Tony. I'm not free this evening, but I'd love to meet up to discuss things. Let me know what you think.*

A whooshing sound came from the computer as the message sent. Though I knew better, I stole another glance at the clock — only five minutes had passed. Annoyed and desperate for something to occupy my time, I fired up a game of Solitaire on my computer and hoped Mitch didn't catch me between now and five o'clock.

☾

I LEFT the Messenger at five o'clock on the dot without saying goodbye to anyone, not even Flora. Nothing was going to get in my way. I charged up Crescent Street and practically ran the few blocks north to Moonbeam Avenue, a stitch in my side by the time I got to number three. I couldn't tell if Raina was home, but either way, I didn't care.

Gingerly, I knocked on the door.

"Be right there," Grandma called, her chair creaking as she stood. A few seconds later, she opened the door just a crack to see who was there and smiled when she realized it was me.

"Dang, you didn't waste no time at all, did ya?" Grandma asked as she opened the door the rest of the way to let me inside. I gave her a hug and when we parted I found Raina sitting in one of the rocking chairs next to Grandma's, Tierney and her lap. The fluffy cat hissed at me but Raina shushed him.

"Good evening, dear," Raina said, smiling.

"Hey, good to see you," I said, though I wasn't sure I meant it. I couldn't shake the feeling I'd walked onto the scene of an intervention and Raina and Grandma were about to tell me all the ways my bad behavior affected them.

"Have a seat," Grandma said as she closed the door and ushered me further into the house. I left the middle of the three rocking chairs for her and sat down on her left.

"I have to say, I don't know what to expect here," I said. Grandma groaned as she lowered herself into the rocking chair and Raina smiled at me.

"Nor do we," Raina said.

"Let's just get right down to the nitty gritty, shall we?" Grandma asked. I nodded, the suspense killing me. I'd been waiting all afternoon to hear whatever it was she had to say.

"Alrighty then, I reckon I'll start at the beginning. Not long after I got here, Raina and I sort of hit it off talking about this that and the other thing," Grandma started.

"Right. You've never met a person you couldn't talk to, that much isn't new," I said and Grandma fixed me with a disapproving look. Raina chuckled.

"Anyway, durin' that process, somethin' sorta stuck out as not really makin' much sense," Grandma said and my body tensed.

"Like what?"

Grandma and Raina exchanged looks and Raina nodded as if to tell her it was okay. My heart hammered so fast I thought it might burst out of my chest and run away.

"Look, I don't know how else to tell ya this, Sugar, so I'm just gonna say it: I dunno whether or not your parents are actually gone," Grandma said. I blinked a few times at her, my brain unable to process what she'd just said.

"I don't understand," I said.

"While she's been here, your grandmother and I have been exploring your family's history as a matter of understanding where you came from and where you might be going," Raina said. "Of course, I've already shared with her the extraordinary progress you've made in your own journey in your studies of magic."

"Minus the part where I got kicked out of school and my wand was taken," I said.

"I was there for that one, Sugar," Grandma said and I shook my head.

"I've also already informed your grandmother that your family descends from quite an impressive line of witches and warlocks, potentially including Lilith, the Prime Witch herself," Raina said.

None of this was news to me; Raina and I had talked it over quite extensively in the time we'd spent together while she was tutoring me in magic.

"Right, so far I'm following you. But why do I get the feeling we're about to hit a road bump?" I asked.

"Because we are. See, here's the thing. It's true that your parents are gone, I just ain't got a clue where they went," Grandma said and my head spun.

"That doesn't make any sense. How can they be gone without you knowing where they went?"

"It's complicated, and that's why I kept it from ya all this time. I kept waitin' for the right time to tell ya but the right time just never came. Now that I'm here and gettin' whiplash from seein' all this magical stuff, I can't deny the truth no more," Grandma said.

My heart hammered in my ears, my blood crashing against the inside of my skull like the waves of the ocean on the shore.

"Just tell me. After all I've come up against here, I think I can handle it," I lied — I wasn't at all sure I could handle it.

"All right, but you can't say I didn't warn ya," Grandma sighed. Raina reached over to squeeze her hand reassuringly, though Grandma wasn't really the one in need of comfort at the moment.

"I think all that bullhockey I been feedin' ya fer years about your parents passin' away in a car crash is just that: bullhockey," Grandma said.

It should have been more shocking than it was, but it wasn't the first time I'd wondered if Grandma wasn't telling me the truth about what really happened to my parents. After all, there was a funeral but there weren't any bodies. Grandma said that was because they were too damaged in the crash, but I never believed it.

"Okay, then what happened?" I asked. Grandma looked like she was stunned I wasn't more upset.

"That's the trouble, I ain't got a clue, and the police don't neither," Grandma said. "It's the darndest thing, Sugar, they just disappeared into thin air."

"But that's not possible. Even if there was some magic or something at work, they would've had to show up somewhere. Not even witches can just make themselves disappear forever, can they?" I asked, looking to Raina for the answer.

"Not as far as I know," Raina said.

"Wait, back up, I feel like I'm missing a lot here. The police didn't find anything at all?" I asked, my head spinning.

"Well, it wasn't *nothin'* they found. Your parents did go on a date together that night, that much about the story is true. But they didn't come home when they said they were gonna. At the time, I didn't think nothin' of it cuz you was still a baby and I knew it'd been a hot Carolina minute since they'd had some time alone," Grandma said.

"But?" I asked. Grandma sighed.

"The next mornin' I still hadn't heard a peep from either of 'em, so I started to get worried. 'Course, this was back in the days before cell phones, so it wasn't like I could call 'em up. Anyway, when the afternoon rolled around and I still hadn't heard nothin', I called the police and filed a missin' persons report," Grandma said.

"And what did they find?" I asked though I wasn't sure I wanted to know the answer.

"They found your father's car abandoned not far down the street from my farm," Grandma said and my heart plunged into my stomach.

"Neither of 'em was in the car and it didn't look like there'd been any sorta struggle. The cops tried to start the car but she wouldn't turn over, so for a long time there the police figured it musta broke down and your parents to walk the rest of the way but never made it home."

"Then where did they go? I mean, if they never made it back to the farm and the police never found anything, they could still be alive, right?" I asked, still unable to believe the things I'd heard.

"I ain't got a clue. The cops kept searchin' for about a week, but you know how it goes with things like that. After a while, they gave up because they didn't find nothin' conclusive," Grandma said. "But then the investigators took the car in fer the black light search or whatever and found something in the glovebox. It was a long, knotted stick."

"Wait, was it a wand?" I asked and Raina smiled at me.

"That's exactly what I thought too," Raina said.

"Fer all I know, it mighta been. There was always somethin' a little off about those two, somethin' I couldn't put my finger on. They were marching to the beat of their own drum or whatever," Grandma said.

"But you said there were no signs of a struggle. If the car broke down, and if they were able to use magic in some capacity, why didn't they take the wand with them if they abandoned the car?" I asked.

"Says the true journalist," Grandma laughed. "That's the thing, I dunno. I wish I had the answers, Sugar, but I don't. I been tryin' to figure it out for twenty-some-odd years. It never made no sense to me either."

"So all this time you've been telling me they were dead, they weren't?" I asked.

"Well, I wouldn't go jumpin' to that conclusion just yet," Grandma said. "Just because we can't find 'em don't mean they're still around."

"None of this makes any sense," I said, slouching back in the rocking chair before I fainted.

"I know, Zoe, I'm sorry. To her credit, your grandmother didn't want to tell you any of this because she knew it would upset you," Raina said. She had that right.

"But I thought it was important for you to know. I can't say with any certainty but based on this story and some records I've found, I have a strong suspicion your parents may have been attempting to get back into Moon Grove," Raina said and I bolted up in the chair again.

"Wait a second, what do you mean back into Moon Grove? That implies they were ever here in the first place," I said. Raina smiled and nodded.

"That's correct," she said. "While talking things over with your grandmother, I learned your mother's maiden name is Woods, the same as mine."

"Okay, but that could just be a coincidence," I said, though my anxiety doubled.

"It could, but there's only one Ember Woods in all of Moon Grove's recorded history. Such are the benefits of having a unique name like your mother's," Raina said.

"What did you find out about her?"

"A birth record for you, among other things. Ember Woods, your mother, gave birth to an unnamed child twenty-five years ago at Willowvale Hospital. The father is listed as Robert Clarke, your father," Raina said. My head threatened to float off my shoulders.

I was born in Moon Grove? To a relative of Raina and Circe? How had we not figured any of this out until now?

"According to the records, your parents weren't yet married when you were born," Raina said.

"That's true, they didn't get married until about a year later," Grandma said, stroking her chin. I'd forgotten she was there.

"Which explains why we were unable to find anything substantive until now. We were looking for the wrong name in all the wrong places," Raina said.

"But why would they leave? They had to have known what life would be like outside the safe zone of Moon Grove for magical folks," I said.

"I suspect because they had you. Maybe they wanted you to have a relationship with your grandmother and a normal childhood, or as normal as they could provide until your magic awoke," Raina said.

"Do you think that's why they tried to come back? Was I showing magical signs even at that young of an age?" I asked.

"Again, based on your lineage and what I've seen you do with your magic since you've gotten here, I wouldn't be surprised in the slightest," Raina said.

"But what about my father? Was he magical too?" I asked.

"Please," Grandma scoffed. "Don't get me wrong, I love the boy to death, but that idjit was about as magical as my big toe." Raina snorted.

If that was true, I wondered what he thought of my mother's abilities — or if my mother hid them from him until after my powers started manifesting in ways she couldn't excuse.

"Do you think he knew about Mom's magic then?"

"Who the heck knows? Until your mother got pregnant, I didn't really see hide nor hair of your parents," Grandma said. "They moved out of Lumberton to Charlotte, or so they said, but I never got invited to their house or nothin' so I dunno if they really lived there or not. They coulda been livin' here for all I know."

"But you never had any clue either or both of them were magical?" I asked Grandma. She shrugged.

"I mean, sure, strange things happened around your mother, but I always took 'em as a coinkydink," Grandma said.

"Like what?"

"Just lil' things. She always seemed to be one step ahead of me like she was readin' my mind or somethin'," Grandma said.

"That sounds familiar," Raina said, smiling at me.

"Whaddya mean?" Grandma asked.

"She probably *was* reading your mind, Grandma," I said. "I can do it too."

"Oh, how lovely. I don't really wanna think about what kinda trouble that could get me in," Grandma said, blushing. I chuckled.

"But what about my mother's parents then? Who were they?" I asked Raina. Raina sighed and shook her head.

"That's the one missing link. There's no birth record for an Ember Woods here, which probably means she was born elsewhere," Raina said.

"You mean in another magical community?"

"Possibly, or in the non-magical realm," Raina said. "Though rare, it does happen from time to time."

"Raina and I have talked this over 'till I was blue in the face lookin' fer other details. I dunno anything about your mother's family, Sugar. I never met 'em, she never talked about 'em. It was almost like she didn't want 'em to exist," Grandma said.

Maybe she didn't. If they weren't magical, she might've been embarrassed by them, or maybe they'd rejected her when they'd learned who and what she was. Had she woken up one day to magic slapping her in the face like I had? Or was it like the slow creep of puberty, the changes growing more and more evident until she couldn't hide them anymore?

I might never know, and that was the hardest part to accept.

Grandma reached for my hand, startling me, and when I looked up she was smiling at me somberly.

"I'm sorry, Sugar. I know this is a lot to lay on ya, but I couldn't keep it from ya no more. It didn't feel right now that you're here and learnin' all this magic and whatnot. You need to know who and what your family is," Grandma said. I squeezed her hand.

"It's okay. It's a lot to process, but I'm glad you told me," I said. "It clears so many things up."

"I reckoned it might."

"Zoe, now that we have your grandmother here and we know who to look for in the records, we'll find more information. I'm sure of it," Raina said.

"Right, of course," I said, hearing my words from outside myself. I needed some air to clear my head. I had so many questions but I knew none of them had answers so I bit them back.

"You okay?" Grandma asked. I nodded.

"I'm fine, I'm just overwhelmed," I said.

"Maybe we should leave things here for now," Raina suggested.

"Good idea," I said. I sat staring at the wall, unable to think straight.

"You sure you're okay, Sugar? I don't want you to—"

An explosion tore through Raina's house, cutting Grandma off. It shook all four walls, rattled dust from the ceiling, and rocked our chairs in the aftershocks. Tierney howled and darted under the nearby sofa, leaving scratch marks on Raina's arms.

"What in Lilith's name was that?" Raina asked as she stood and hurried to the window to look outside. I was on her heels, but I couldn't see anything. Frustrated, I tore out of the house and a hand automatically clapped over my mouth when I saw all-too-familiar green flames hundreds of feet away licking and lashing at the darkness — in the vicinity of Hypnotic Tonics.

Another fire was the last thing I needed.

"Stay here, Grandma!" I shouted.

"Are you pullin' my leg? I survived them green flames once, I ain't gettin' nowhere near 'em again!" Grandma shouted back.

"Zoe, wait!" Raina called and reached for my arm to stop me, but I yanked it away and dashed down Moonbeam Avenue toward Crescent Street, desperate to get to Hypnotic Tonics before anyone else did.

CHAPTER THIRTEEN

GLASS POPPED and liquid sizzled as a roaring emerald blaze consumed Hypnotic Tonics. The windows were blown out, the lawn littered with glass, and even the yard ornaments were melting like candles on a cake.

I felt helpless, not for the first time since coming to Moon Grove. Thanks to the flame spreading like a contagion and my lack of a wand to defend myself, I didn't dare get too close. Still, I couldn't stop thinking about Hilda and Sage trapped inside.

What on earth happened? Had one of their alchemical experiments gone wrong? It was the only explanation I could think of, but that didn't mean it was the right one. Regardless, the police and the magic medics would be on the scene in a matter of seconds, so I had to act fast if I wanted to find anything that might point me in the right direction.

Careful to avoid touching anything that was already ablaze, I darted around the building to the back and gasped when I saw Sage on hands and knees. Coughs racked her entire body like her lungs were on fire as she crawled away from the shop.

I ran to her and had just crouched down when another explosion rocked the building and sent me tumbling backward into the grass. Dazed but determined, I forced myself back up and wrapped Sage's arm around my shoulder to carry her away. Her feet dragged in the grass and her head lolled against my shoulder, but somehow I managed to get her to safety.

Together, we slumped down into the grass under a tree some thirty feet away from the raging flames. I watched in horror as the frame of the building collapsed in on itself, belching a gust of scalding air and green embers onto the nearby buildings. If the firefighters and police didn't arrive soon, the entire street might burn down.

"Zoe?" Sage coughed as she stirred back to life.

"Yes, it's me. Are you okay?" I asked, frantic.

"I think so," she croaked, rubbing her throat that must've gone raw from smoke inhalation.

"Do you remember what happened? Anything at all?" I asked.

"No, I was working in the back room and the next thing I know everything's on fire," Sage said. Then her eyes went wide and she tried to claw away from me back toward the store. "Hilda! She's still in there, we have to do something!"

I seized her robes, which were charred and reeked of smoke, to hold her back. The last thing I needed was for her to go Rambo trying to save someone who was most likely already gone.

"Sage, no! It's too dangerous, we have to wait for the fire department," I said. Sage let out a howl somewhere between crying and anguish until her voice went out. She fell back into my arms. "You have to tell me if you saw anything. It can make the difference here."

"I swear, I didn't. I was in the back room taking stock of everything we needed to replace after the day's sales and then everything turned to fire," Sage said, tears glistening in her eyes thanks to the eerie green light from the fire.

"What was Hilda doing?" I asked.

"I don't know. I think maybe she was working on a new formula. We've been toying around with a new recipe for the last few days," Sage said.

"What kind of formula?"

"The kind to put out fires like this," Sage sobbed as she realized the irony of it all. "After the horrible fire at Councilman Woods' house, Hilda was obsessed with creating something that could put that kind of fire out if it ever happened again."

Her words twisted in my side like a knife.

"You said you were having trouble with it. What kind of trouble?"

"It was volatile. We tested it in the smallest batches possible first in a magically-controlled environment in case anything right wrong, so I don't know what happened, but it must've been an accident. It had to have been an accident," Sage said.

I opened my mouth to ask another question but didn't get the chance because a gang of witches and warlocks in red robes rocketed overhead, their wands drawn and held at the ready as they formed a circle around the blaze. Fire Chief Blaine Hart was at the front of the group and I took some small comfort in knowing he'd dealt with this recently and knew which mistakes not to make twice.

"Are they going to save her?" Sage muttered, several of her fingers between her teeth.

"They'll do everything they can," I said, though I didn't have much hope. If it was true Hilda was in the middle of the shop working on a formula when the explosion happened, surrounded by all the other combustible formulas on sale...

"I don't believe this," Sage said. That made two of us. I hoped against all hope that this latest fire was truly the result of an accident, but it didn't look that way. Circe's house had been deliberately torched by Wild Fyre and it couldn't have been a coincidence that Hypnotic Tonics was now alight with the same contagious green flames.

"Are you sure it was an accident?" I asked. Sage pushed out of my arms to glare at me.

"Are you saying what I think you're saying?" she shouted, her face twisted in anger. "Why on earth would Hilda set her own shop on fire?" Sage asked.

That wasn't what I meant, though it was an interesting theory. Hilda did owe a lot of money to Tony, so what if she decided to burn the place to cinders so she'd never have to pay it back? Or better yet, what if she had some sort of insurance policy on the shop she was trying to collect? People had done crazier things than this for an insurance payout.

"Good question," I said.

"Listen to yourself, you sound crazy!" Sage said. She pointed at the blaze and the firefighters swarming around it. "Who would do this to themselves?"

"Well, maybe it wasn't her," I said, looking Sage directly in the eye. She stared back like she didn't understand, but when it clicked she looked like she might lunge at me.

"You think *I* did this?! I nearly died!" Sage's shouted.

"I didn't say that. I just raised the question," I said.

"And that's about all you're good at, isn't it? Trouble is, you're asking all the wrong ones," Sage said. "Meanwhile, my entire livelihood is burning to the ground and my mentor is probably dead."

"What do you mean?" I asked.

"This was Hilda's entire life, and I wanted nothing more than to follow in her footsteps. I would never have thought about hurting her or the shop," Sage said.

"Okay, then who did? I already know you and Hilda had some unsavory connections, to say the least," I said."I know Hilda owes Tony Romano a lot of money to pay back the loan she got from him to open the shop."

Sage looked like a deer in emerald headlights as the fire raged in the whites of her eyes.

"You obviously already know, so there's no sense in denying it. That part's true," Sage said. "But I don't think it was Tony who did this, not after what happened today."

"Which was?"

"Tony isn't the only one Hilda owes money to for the shop," Sage said, staring at me like she was looking right through me.

"Who else?" I demanded, crawling closer to make sure I heard.

"Lorelei Riddle," Sage said. The fire roared as it consumed the last remnants of Hypnotic Tonics but still couldn't drown out the din of the thousands of thoughts running through my head.

"What?"

"You heard me. Lorelei Riddle, the same Councilwoman who was intent on making sure we never opened our shop, gave Hilda money for what she considered research and development," Sage said.

"Her family's loaded, but given the legal trouble her daughter's in no thanks to you, money's drying up fast. So Lorelei gave Hilda a startup loan in exchange for a slice of the future profits," she continued.

"I don't understand. Why would Lorelei give you money and then try to shut you down?" I asked.

"Maybe she got scared word was going to get out. She came into the shop earlier today shouting. She wanted to know how you found out about her breathing down our necks, and she wasn't happy when I told her you'd come in poking for information," Sage said.

My throat tightened. If Lorelei came into Hypnotic Tonics to put the squeeze on Hilda and Sage, that meant she was afraid of me and the questions I was asking — but why?

Probably because she didn't want me to find out she had financial ties to Hilda and Hypnotic Tonics. I wasn't intimately familiar with the laws and regulations in Moon Grove, but I found it hard to believe there weren't any prohibitions against Council members investing in businesses that could create a conflict of interest.

"Why are you just telling me now about Lorelei's loan to Hilda? Don't you think I might've liked to know that sooner?" I asked.

"Because I knew you thought Hilda killed Circe, and I wanted to protect her. I was sure that once you got on the trail of whoever was actually responsible for the fire, you'd leave us alone," Sage said.

"And you think Lorelei is the one responsible for both of these fires?" I asked.

"Her daughter is a convicted murderer, so I wouldn't be surprised," Sage said.

A chill rippled through my entire body and Sage fell silent as she watched the firefighters desperately trying to stop the fire from spreading. They flitted around the blaze like moths to a flame, never close enough to touch it, but close enough to make me worry.

Hilda was in much more debt than I knew. Tony wasn't lying when he told me he suspected Hilda owed money to people other than him, but I never would've guessed Lorelei Riddle had a role in any of this.

Did she just think the shop's profits would be a quick way to refill her coffers when she agreed to give Hilda the money — and then had second thoughts when the business came under scrutiny? Or was there something else going on? It was next to impossible to say.

Fire Chief Blaine Hart touched down in front of us. He held his broomstick in one hand and it was so small next to his massive, muscular frame that it looked like a child's toy.

"Zoe, what are you doing here? Are you okay?" he asked, recognizing me immediately. I nodded.

"I'm fine, but I'm not so sure about her," I said. "This is Sage Snow, she's the apprentice in the shop."

"Have you saved Hilda? Is she okay? I need to see her," Sage said, borderline hysterical. "I don't know what I'll do if she doesn't come out of there."

Blaine looked at me with concern on his face and I knew it was too late. Hilda was gone.

"I'm sorry, Ms. Snow, but I don't think there's anything we can do at this point," Blaine said and Sage howled. I wrapped my arms around her and Blaine regarded us like he didn't have any idea what to do.

"You always seem to be in the wrong place at the wrong time, Zoe," Blaine said. Yeah, no kidding. "Did you see anything?"

"No, I felt the explosion from a few blocks away while I was visiting with my grandmother and I ran here as fast as I could. I found Sage crawling through the grass and helped her get away," I said.

"And what about you, Ms. Snow? Did you see anything before the fire started?" Blaine asked. I held my breath and waited to hear whether or not the story Sage told him would match the one she'd told me.

"No. I was working in the back room when all of a sudden there as a booming sound and everything turned green. It knocked me down and I crawled my way outside," Sage said. "But it had to have been an accident, some tonic or another gone wrong."

That wasn't what Sage implied to me. Maybe Lorelei Riddle had decided she wasn't going to make her investment back and needed a way to get rid of the evidence that she'd ever been involved with Hypnotic Tonics in the first place.

"I understand. We need to get you both away from here, it's not safe," Blaine said and motioned to one of the other firefighters who was still circling the blaze and casting protective spells on nearby buildings to keep the fire from spreading.

A witch with long dark hair soared out of the air and landed beside us. She smiled at us like everything was going to be okay, but I had a hard time believing that.

"This is Lena, one of my best crew members. She's going to fly you both to the hospital," Blaine said.

But as he spoke, a flash of red and blue lights mixed with the green of the fire and I sighed as I realized the police had finally arrived — and though I had no idea what took them so long, after everything Sage told me I was grateful they'd dragged their feet. Still, if I knew Police Chief Mueller half as well as I thought I did, there was no way he'd let anyone take Sage anywhere until he got her story on record.

"Or maybe not," Blaine sighed, eyeing the police cruiser as it squeaked to a stop along Crescent Street. Mueller and Officer Ewan Barrett, Flora's boyfriend, stepped out of the vehicle. Both wore grim expressions as they stared at the blaze.

"Why am I not surprised to see you here?" Mueller asked me as he raked his eyes over us.

"Believe it or not, I didn't have anything to do with this one," I said.

"That's what you always say," Mueller said, though the hint of a smile appeared on his droopy, hound-like face.

"I wasn't far away when I heard the explosion so I ran over here to help," I said.

"Right, to help, of course," Mueller said, his eyes twinkling.

"It's a good thing she did, otherwise Ms. Snow here might not have been so lucky," Blaine said, nodding at Sage.

"You know, Chief Hart, this fire looks an awful lot like the last one."

"They're the same, no doubt about it. We don't know how it started yet, but—"

"It was an accident, I'm telling you!" Sage shouted, interrupting them. Why was she so intent on convincing the authorities of that when she'd suggested to me Lorelei might've started it? Was she trying to cover for Lorelei, or was she giving me a head start to find out why?

Maybe Sage trusted me more to get to the truth than she did Mueller or anyone else in law enforcement. Based on their track record since I'd gotten to town, I couldn't say I blamed her.

"Well, save your story because you're going to have to repeat it anyway when we get to the station," Mueller said as he hitched his pants up by his belt. He'd lost weight and his face was more rugged than usual, no doubt both a result of everything going on in town lately.

"I strongly suggest you have Ms. Snow looked at by a medical professional first. She's had extensive exposure to smoke and Lilith knows what other airborne chemicals," Blaine said and Mueller side-eyed him.

"We have the resources at the station, don't worry," Mueller said. Blaine shrugged and stepped back like he wasn't about to contradict Mueller. "Load her up, Barrett," Mueller ordered and Ewan launched into action. Gently, he crouched down to help Sage off the ground.

"We've gotta stop meeting like this," Ewan whispered to me and I smiled. "All right, up you go, Ms. Snow," he said as he hoisted Sage to her feet. He winked at me and walked her to the police cruiser.

When they were gone, Mueller turned his focus to me.

"She tell you anything? Or, did you, erm, *hear* anything?" Mueller asked, an obvious reference to my ability to hear people's thoughts. Unfortunately for me, I hadn't had the wits to think about reading Sage's mind while she was still around, but I didn't think she was hiding anything anyway.

"No, not really. She swore she was minding her business doing inventory work when the shop exploded. She did say that she thinks it was an experimental formula gone wrong though," I said.

Mueller stared at me like he knew I wasn't telling him everything, but I wasn't about to give away my best lead to him or anyone else.

"I might not know much about witchcraft, but I'm pretty sure there's no formula that could've backfired and created something like this," Mueller said. I'd thought the same thing. "If you find anything else, let me know."

"Of course," I said. Mueller nodded and walked off toward the police cruiser, leaving Blaine and his crew to deal with the fire. If it was anything like the last one, they'd probably have to do their best to contain it until it ran out of tinder and suffocated itself.

"I better get back to it. But between you and me, there's no way this was an accident," Blaine said as he mounted his broom.

"I know," I said. Blaine nodded and kicked off the ground, leaving me with nothing but his dust and thoughts of Lorelei Riddle swimming through my mind.

CHAPTER FOURTEEN

HEAD WARLOCK HEATH HIGHMORE'S gavel slammed against its sound block, silencing everyone in the room. The Council had called an emergency meeting to discuss the fire at Hypnotic Tonics, and even if I hadn't been directly tied to the incident, I would've made sure Mitch allowed me to cover it — and to get face time with Lorelei.

"Fellow citizens of Moon Grove," Heath said from where he stood on the raised dais, his magically-amplified voice bouncing off the walls of the cavernous town hall. "It brings me no pleasure to assemble you all today."

Grunts and grumbles from the audience of reporters and townsfolk responded, but I was glued to my seat in the front row, pen and paper at the ready. Beau sat beside me smiling warmly as the room settled, probably grateful it wasn't me facing questioning this time. I'd caught him up on everything before the start of the meeting.

Lorelei sat at the left edge of the other Council members, straight-backed and stern while she avoided my eyes. Of everyone in front of me, she was the one I cared about most — and come spell or high water, I needed to get her alone at some point.

"As you may or may not know, Hypnotic Tonics burned last night," Heath continued over the last rustlings of people getting situated. "It is with great mourning I must report that Hilda Blackwood, the shop's owner, passed away in the blaze."

Crickets. Either no one remembered who Hilda was or they just thought she was a crazy old hippy not worth caring about — or both.

Though I didn't dare turn around to check, I felt dozens of pairs of eyeballs on the back of my head. No doubt word had gotten around that I was at the scene, but I was just doing my job.

"In an effort to communicate the circumstances to you and to further understand the situation, I've invited Sage Snow, Hilda's shop assistant and apprentice, to join us to answer some questions this afternoon," Heath said as he sat down and scooted his chair up to the dais.

My eyes flitted to Sage, who sat in the same chair I'd occupied less than a week ago when all of Moon Grove's scrutiny was laser-focused on me. Though Sage had done her makeup before the meeting, it'd already run down her face with her tears and the sleeves of her violet robes were stained where she'd wiped herself clean. Her hair laid loosely across her shoulders, tangled and unbrushed.

It was difficult not to feel sorry for her.

"Ms. Snow, thank you for joining us," Heath said. Sage nodded without saying anything; she didn't have much choice in the matter.

"Before we get started, I want to be clear in stating that this meeting is simply that: a meeting. You aren't in any danger, legal or otherwise, by being here. The Council only seeks information," Heath said. Again, Sage nodded.

"I understand," she said, her trembling voice barely audible.

"Good. Please begin by telling us the first thing you can remember about last night," Heath said.

"It was mundane. Hilda and I had just finished closing the shop for the night and I was in the storeroom taking inventory like I always do at the end of the day," Sage said.

"Inventory? I assume that means so you know what more to produce?" Heath asked.

"Yes, sir," Sage answered. "Nothing is outsourced. All of our tonics are made by hand."

"Impressive, and good to know. So, you didn't see or hear anything out of the ordinary before the shop caught fire?" Heath asked. Sage stared at Lorelei and though Lorelei never moved, I felt her crawling out of her skin.

"No, nothing," Sage said. I knew she was lying — or at least she was based on what she'd told me about Lorelei storming into the shop — but what was I supposed to say? I couldn't prove it anyway and the Council had heard more than enough from me lately.

"I see. Then what do you think happened to cause a fire like the one last night?" Heath asked.

"I'm not sure, sir, but I have a suspicion. Hilda and I have been working on a new tonic, something that could put out fires like last night's, but we haven't been able to perfect it."

"What was wrong with it, if I may ask?" Heath asked. Sage shrugged.

"It was just as unpredictable as the fire it was designed to contain," Sage said. She seemed oddly comfortable talking about it.

"Then do you think that could have been what caused the fire?" Heath asked.

"Yes. But it just as easily could've been something or someone else," Sage said, her eyes locked on Lorelei. My entire body went rigid. Was Sage really about to implicate Lorelei in front of all her peers?

"Such as?" Heath asked.

"Her," Sage said, jabbing a finger at Lorelei, who looked like she might explode. "Everyone knows she never wanted our shop to open."

"That's a ridiculous accusation and far out of order," Lorelei spat as she slammed her palms against the dais. "The only thing I was concerned about was making sure the consumers of your tonics were safe. Clearly, I had reason to worry."

"No, the only thing you cared about was your bottom line," Sage snapped. Heath's brows furrowed and all the Council members looked at Lorelei as she sputtered.

"She's inventing stories to distract from her own culpability," Lorelei said as she flipped her blonde hair over her shoulders.

"Is she?" Councilwoman Bloodworth asked, hunched over the dais to look Lorelei in the eye. She pushed her oversized glasses up her hooked nose with a trembling hand and waited for an answer.

"She is," Lorelei said as if that settled it.

"No, I'm not," Sage interrupted. "Councilwoman Riddle gave Hilda a loan to start Hypnotic Tonics in exchange for a slice of the profits and got scared of being found out when people started asking questions."

Well, the cat was out of the bag now.

An audible gasp tore through the town hall and turned into a roar of conversation. Was this why Sage didn't tell Mueller about Lorelei? If she wanted attention cast on Lorelei's involvement, it'd worked. Heath slammed his gavel down several times to bring order back to the room.

"That's a serious accusation, Ms. Snow," Heath said.

"It is, and I would've had proof via the contract they signed if the Councilwoman hadn't burned our shop to the ground," Sage said to another roar of reactions. Stunned, I scribbled a note and elbowed Beau. His eyes were as wide as full moons.

"If there were a contract, you'd have a copy yourself, would you not, Councilwoman?" Heath asked Lorelei. She squirmed in her seat.

"No, because there is no contract. She's lying," Lorelei said, flustered, but it didn't seem that way to me. Where Lorelei couldn't sit still, Sage was like a rock: firm and unmoving while she stared at Lorelei.

Heath didn't look like he believed her either. Still, he must've known this wasn't leading to anything productive because he hammered the sound block with his gavel again.

"Based on this new information, I'm afraid we must call a close to this meeting for the time being while we re-evaluate," Heath said to shouts of disapproval. "Ms. Snow, we'll need to keep you in custody for now, as I'm sure you understand."

Sage nodded as two of the Council's gargoyle guards approached to escort her out of the room.

I couldn't blame anyone in the room for being upset — I wanted information just as much as they did, and if they weren't willing to give it to us voluntarily, I'd just have to weasel it out of them.

Lorelei shoved back from the dais and set off in a hurry toward the exit without saying a word to any of her colleagues. I bolted up and tossed my pad of paper on the chair behind me to intercept her before she had the chance to get away for good.

"Zoe, what are you doing?!" Beau shouted after me, but I ignored him. Lorelei had just reached the bottom of the dais' stairs when I blocked her path, my arms crossed. Her face twisted and she made to step around me but I moved with her.

"Get out of my way, Ms. Clarke, or I'll have you removed," Lorelei said and as if they'd been waiting, I felt stone-cold air rolling off the skin of two of another pair of gargoyle guards. Though a chill ripped through me and my heart fluttered in my chest, I wasn't going to be intimidated by her or anyone else.

"Look, you can either talk to me now and keep some amount of control over the story or you can let it run away from you with speculation at the reins. Your choice," I said.

Lorelei fumed, but as more people approached shouting questions, she nodded to the gargoyles. They carved a path for us through the sea of residents and held steady as we fought through to Lorelei's office.

With the two of us safely inside, the gargoyles slammed the door shut and the noise from outside ceased as if we'd stepped into a vacuum. Were the doors magically sealed to protect whatever the Council members wanted to talk about inside?

"This is unbelievable," Lorelei mumbled as she stepped around the various boxes lying on the floor. It looked like she hadn't been in the office long — or if she had she hadn't done a very good job of unpacking.

She collapsed into the tired, torn office chair behind her littered desk and held her head in her hands. I'd never seen Lorelei so out of sorts before, not even when I showed up at her house. Like her daughter, Lorelei was normally as cold and hard as steel, but sitting across from me at that moment she just looked broken.

"Is it true?" I asked, and she jumped like she'd forgotten I was there. She looked me in the eyes like she was looking through me rather than at me.

"Is what true?" she asked.

"Your loan to Hilda for Hypnotic Tonics," I said. She withered in her chair and slowly nodded her head.

"It is," Lorelei said. "I can't believe I'm telling you of all people this, but yes, it's true," she laughed, her hands thrown in the air.

"Then was it you who firebombed the store? I know you were there yesterday demanding to know why Sage and Hilda had talked to me," I said. No sense in beating around the bush.

"Are you serious? If I gave someone my last few dollars to open up a shop with the expectation of making more money back, why would I blow it all up?" she asked. She had a point, but wait, her last few dollars? What reasonable person loaned all of their savings to an unproven business — and why?

"More than that, I'm a newly-appointed member of the Council who's already under scrutiny thanks to my daughter's actions. My family's reputation has suffered enough. I wouldn't dream of doing anything to bring draw further suspicion on us," she said.

"Then why did you strike a deal you had to know was a major conflict of interest?" I asked.

"I wasn't yet on the Council when Hilda and I made the deal," Lorelei said.

"But didn't you think it was a good idea to disclose that deal when you were appointed, just to be safe?" I asked.

"No. The other Council members would never have voted to confirm my appointment if they knew," Lorelei said.

"Confirm you? How did you get on the Council anyway?" I asked. I'd always wondered since there wasn't an election.

"I was appointed. It's rare, but the Head Witch and Warlock both have the power to bypass an election by appointing someone to the Council in the case of an emergency," Lorelei said.

Then why would Heath choose Lorelei of all people? He seemed far too cautious not to have noticed something was off about her — like the fact that her daughter was in jail for murdering a teacher and a fellow student.

"Why didn't the Council announce it? I had no idea you'd joined them until I came before you recently," I said.

"Heath didn't want to make a scene of it. There's been enough commotion politically and otherwise in this town, the last thing he wanted was to create more," Lorelei said. Well, again, he sure chose an odd candidate for that goal.

"He's not wrong. Anyway, why did you make a deal with Hilda in the first place? You don't seem like the impulsive type."

"No, far from it under normal circumstances," Lorelei laughed. "But these are hardly normal circumstances. My family is broke, Ms. Clarke. I needed a way to make money, desperately, and I thought a small investment in a business that was sure to take off would pay, but none of it matters now because Hypnotic Tonics and Hilda both are cinders."

"How did your family go broke? The Riddles are one of the oldest, richest families in this town," I said.

"Because of you, frankly," Lorelei laughed. "The fines and legal bills involved with defending murderous daughters are quite high, as I'm sure you can imagine."

There wasn't any point in telling her I was sorry because I wasn't. As painful as it must've been for Lorelei and her family to go through, it was much better for Aurelia to be behind bars. She was too dangerous.

But the more I talked to Lorelei, the less I believed she was murderous herself. I walked to her desk and sat down on the corner of it.

"Then where did you get the money to invest in Hilda's shop if you were so broke?" I asked.

"It was the last of the inheritance Claudette left my husband," Lorelei said. "At the rate we were burning through it, I knew the money would be gone in a matter of weeks. I thought I could make the last of it work for me by striking a deal with Hilda to share her profits, which I thought would be astronomical, but Lilith was I ever wrong."

"I'm confused. You loaned Hilda money so she could start her shop, but then somewhere along the way you became her biggest obstacle. What happened?" I asked.

"Hilda happened," Lorelei laughed. "I should've known better than to go into business with someone so disorganized."

"Was the business not doing well?" I asked. I already had the answer to that, but I wanted to hear it from her mouth.

"The problem started long before the business opened," Lorelei said. "It became clear to me very early on that Hilda had no idea what it took to get a business off the ground, much less turn it into a successful money maker."

"How so?"

"Thanks to its legacy and age, there are strict restrictions on opening new stores and services within Moon Grove's borders so new ventures are inspected and regulated within inches of their lives," Lorelei said.

"Interesting."

"More like infuriating, but thanks to my prior career as a businesswoman I've been around the regulation block a few times, so I thought I could help Hilda through the process. But each time she was inspected, she was either unprepared, a no-show, or fell flat on her face. I started to worry the shop would get shut down before it ever opened so I decided to try to, well, *motivate* her and Sage a bit more," Lorelei said.

By that, she meant antagonizing them, but I couldn't say I blamed her. If my entire family's future were riding on someone like Hilda, I might've done the same thing.

"But Hypnotic Tonics eventually opened, so there had to have been money coming in at some point, right?" I asked. Lorelei shook her head.

"There was certainly money being made, but none of it was flowing back to me," Lorelei said as she rummaged in one of her desk drawers. She pulled out a few sheets of paper that were stapled together and shoved them across the desk to me. It was the contract she'd signed with Hilda — which meant she'd lied to the Council and to most of Moon Grove by denying it existed.

"If you look at the last page, you'll see Hilda and I agreed to a ten percent share of any profits made. I saw precisely zero," she said as I thumbed through the sheets. At the bottom of the third page, it was spelled out in bolded letters and clear language.

"But if she wasn't paying you, where was that money going?" I asked.

"That's exactly what I was trying to find out," Lorelei said. "So I hired someone to help me get some answers."

I sat up straight as an arrow on the corner of her desk.

"Who?"

"His name is Marcel Desfleurs. He works for Grave Times officially but does lots of other work on the side. Maybe you've met him?"

"Oh, I've definitely met him," I said, ice trickling down the back of my neck as I spoke. Marcel had lied to me. He wasn't keeping watch on Hypnotic Tonics because he wanted to — Lorelei was paying him.

"Wait, I thought you were broke?" I asked.

"I wasn't paying him with money," Lorelei said and another glacier of ice slid down my back.

"Then how were you paying him?"

"In information. Councilwoman Woods and I were deep in negotiations with the werewolf leadership," Lorelei said. By that, she meant Tony Romano, though I wasn't about to tell her I knew that too.

"You were feeding Marcel insider information about the negotiations with the werewolves, weren't you?" I asked, filling in the blanks. Lorelei nodded so slowly it was almost imperceptible.

"What exactly were the werewolves bargaining for?" I asked.

"A seat at the table. Though we never explicitly offered it, it was implied that by cooperating with us and agreeing not to stir up trouble the werewolves could find themselves in a position of real power for the first time," Lorelei said.

"And you were going to give it to Tony Romano," I said. Lorelei smirked.

"Perhaps you're more talented than I gave you credit for, Ms. Clarke," Lorelei said.

"Thanks, I guess. But why would Marcel care about what was going on in those negotiations?" I asked.

"It wasn't him so much as it was his boss," Lorelei said.

Of course. I hadn't forgotten that Lucien Bellerose, the land barren of Moon Grove and slippery vampire supreme, had once been involved in a power play for a seat on the Council himself. After he'd failed, he'd been lying low — but he clearly hadn't given up yet. Sending Marcel to do his bidding was clever, I had to give him that; no one would be suspicious of a photojournalist for asking questions and taking pictures.

It was obviously time for me to make another trip to the offices of Grave Times.

"Are you going to print any of this?" Lorelei asked as she reached for the contract. She pulled her wand out of her robes and held the tip to the paper, which charred and curled as it ignited.

"The truth will get out one way or another. You can't burn all your secrets," I said.

"I had nothing to do with either of those fires, Zoe, you have to believe me," Lorelei said. "Whatever you might think about my daughter, I'm not like her. I'm ambitious, absolutely, but not like that."

"I know you're not," I said and Lorelei looked like she might cry. She wouldn't have told me any of this if she really had killed Circe and Hilda. She probably wanted to know who was responsible as much as I did — but she had a lot more skin in the game.

"Thank you for the info, Councilwoman, and good luck with everything," I said as I showed myself out of her office.

As sorry as I felt for her, something told me once the truth came out in the ashes, she wouldn't be occupying it for much longer.

CHAPTER FIFTEEN

I STORMED into the office of Lucien Bellerose, not bothering to exercise any caution or tact. Once more, Céline sat at the receptionist desk looking thoroughly bored. I couldn't say I blamed her — after hundreds of years as a secretary, there probably wasn't much of anything that excited her anymore.

"Good evening," she said as I approached.

"Is Marcel in tonight?" I asked, cutting through the pleasantries. I didn't have the time or patience.

"Let me check," Céline said and picked up the phone on her desk. She had a seconds-long conversation with whoever answered and gave me a half-hearted smile as she held the phone away from her ear. "I'm afraid he's busy right now. Is it an emergency?"

"Yes, definitely. It won't be long, I promise," I said. Céline relayed the information and hung up. She smashed the button on her desk and the door to my right flung open. Before I could get to the entrance, Céline was standing next to me.

"I'm never going to get used to that," I said. Céline smirked and ushered me down the hall toward the door that led into the Grave Times workroom. She didn't try to make any banter with me, but I wasn't complaining.

"Here you are," she said and tapped her badge to open the door. Just like last time, Marcel was standing inside waiting for me, though he didn't look happy to see me.

"Hey, Zoe," Marcel said. "I got your email, sorry I haven't responded. I guess it doesn't matter now though, does it?"

"No, not really," I said and closed the door behind me. Marcel crossed his arms over his chest and looked at me sideways, his skin glowing in the light from all the computers in the room.

"Something on your mind? You seem a little, well, intense this evening," Marcel said. Had he really not heard about the drama in the town hall earlier that afternoon? With all his snooping in other people's business — and that was just the stuff I knew about — I found it hard to believe.

"You played me," I said. Marcel laughed and shook his head, his brows creased like he didn't understand.

"I'm sorry?"

"You had an ulterior motive working with me, didn't you?" I asked.

"I'm really not following you," he said.

"The other night, when we went to Pupperoni Pizza to get dirt on Tony, you didn't go just because you wanted to help me, did you?" I asked.

"Well, no, of course not. I don't do anything unless there's something in it for me as well," Marcel said. "I've never led you to believe otherwise."

"That's true. I've learned a lot in the last couple of days, and none of it really makes you look good," I said.

"Pray tell, what exactly did I get out of our little rendezvous?" Marcel asked, his French accent slipping on the last word.

"What you wanted all along: photographic proof to discredit Tony Romano and ruin the negotiations he was working on with Circe Woods and Lorelei Riddle," I said. "And you lied to me about it to make it seem like you were doing me a favor."

"It's true that I saw a golden opportunity with you, and I won't apologize for taking it," Marcel said and I scoffed. He really was just as conniving as his boss.

"You can beat around the bush all you want, but I know you've been working for Lorelei Riddle. That's why you were hanging around Hypnotic Tonics and why you had the photos of Tony inside the shop after hours," I said. "You two were trading information."

"She told you that, did she?" Marcel asked. He seemed genuinely surprised — though I couldn't tell if he was impressed or afraid — either way, it didn't matter. I had the truth now, or at least part of it, and I needed the rest. I wouldn't fall for his slick words and smooth operation again.

"She did, among other things. I can't believe I didn't put two and two together sooner, but it should have been obvious from the start. Lucien Bellerose owns and runs this magazine and he doesn't want anyone other than the vampires coming to power, so I don't doubt for a second that's why you took the job with Lorelei," I said.

"And if I did, would you blame me? I'm hundreds of years old, Zoe, I didn't get this far in life without being a little cold and calculating," Marcel said.

"That's putting it lightly. Based on all this, why should I believe you had nothing to do with torching Circe's house that night? In fact, why should I believe anything you say?" I asked. Marcel opened his mouth to argue, but I talked over him.

"I think Lucien put you up to it when you told him how friendly Circe had gotten with the werewolves!" I shouted. "I saw the way you moved, how quickly and silently, when you were tearing through the woods in the Werewolves' Quarter. You could easily have been running around while the curfew was in place with a tube of Wild Fyre and no one would've seen you."

"Nice try, but you haven't thought this through, Zoe," Marcel said. "First off, where would I have gotten Wild Fyre? I wasn't the one getting tonics on the sly from Hilda, and I've never known a vampire who was eager to cozy up to flames," Marcel said.

Neither had I, but that was beside the point.

"Beyond that, why would I incriminate myself by showing you the photos I'd taken of Tony at Hypnotic Tonics if I was later planning to blow the place up? Wouldn't it have made more sense for me just to light it on fire without telling anyone I'd been hanging around?" Marcel asked.

"Because you were trying to use Tony as a scapegoat. He already looked suspicious after his outburst at the Council meeting and you had the photos to prove he was in some sort of shady deal with Hilda," I said.

Marcel shrugged.

"You knew that discrediting Tony and pinning Circe's murder on him would make all the Council's negotiations with the werewolves fall apart. But you couldn't spread the suspicion about Tony yourself, so you used me to do it while getting even more compromising photos of him," I said.

"When you put it that way, it does sound like a brilliant idea," Marcel said like he hadn't already thought of it.

"And then when the suspicion was out there, you blew up Hypnotic Tonics to take out Hilda and Sage because they were the only ones who knew the truth and their deaths would really make it look like Tony was on a revenge spree," I said.

"But the plan fell apart when Sage Snow survived and came

forward with accusations against Lorelei Riddle. That was when you knew you were busted because Lorelei was in on it too."

"It's unfortunate that Lorelei admitted I was working for her, but at least she only told you," Marcel said. "I would hate for you to spread that around and end up with egg on your face."

"What are you talking about? You can stop pretending, I know what you did," I said.

"No, you have no idea," Marcel said. "Think of me, Lucien, and Grave Times what you will, but none of us is so brazen as to take the lives of our fellow citizens."

"And that's what everyone else would think too, which is why you resorted to the use of Wild Fyre because you knew no one would suspect a vampire of using something like that. I've been in Lucien's office, I know he collects all kinds of ancient books, so it was probably him who made the Wild Fyre in the first place," I said.

Marcel laughed and shook his head.

"I will say, you have an active imagination, Zoe," Marcel said. "But you're wrong on almost every count."

"Then why don't you tell me the truth? All of it," I said.

"Fine. You're on the right track, but you got off too early. Yes, it's true that Mr. Bellerose wasn't happy when he found out the Council was entertaining the werewolves with negotiations," Marcel said. "He saw it as an indirect threat to the advancement of the vampires, and as a personal slight based on his prior negotiations with another member of the Council."

"Opal Cromwell, yeah, I know all about that one," I said. "I was the one who broke the story on that."

"Yes, exactly. So, naturally, Monsieur Bellerose asked me to dig up anything I could to help throw a wrench into those negotiations — and to find out what the werewolves and the Council had agreed on, if anything," Marcel said.

"And?"

"I never got the answer. That's been the problem all along," Marcel said.

"How is that even possible? You're connected to all these people in some way and you've been taking photos of some of them for weeks, so how could you not have found out what was going on behind the scenes?" I asked.

Of all the things he'd told me so far, this was the hardest to believe.

"Now you can imagine my delight when Lorelei came to me and asked for my help," Marcel said. "Finally, I had a way into the inner circle."

"And someone to feed you information straight from the werewolf's mouth," I said. Marcel nodded.

"I thought so too, but nonpayment seems to be a chronic issue in this town because Lorelei never told me anything I didn't already know," Marcel said. "Every time we talked she strung me along with enough vagaries to make me believe she'd eventually have something for me, but she never did."

"Wait, are you saying you don't think she knew anything at all about the negotiations?" I asked, growing more confused by the second.

"No, she definitely knew, I just don't think she wanted to tell me the truth because the negotiations were doomed from the start and were already crumbling by the time Lorelei and I started working together," Marcel said. "All thanks to the Blood Moon and the curfew."

"What?"

"When Tony lost his temper and accused the Council of discrimination, whatever they were working on died right then and there," Marcel said. "And as far as I can tell, Lorelei and Circe were never on the same page when it came to how to handle the werewolves anyway."

"I can believe that. Lorelei doesn't seem like the most open and warm kind of person," I said.

"No. Warm and open people don't exploit others for their own gain by dangling a loan as a carrot on a stick," Marcel said. "But I don't think it was Lorelei who ultimately pulled the plug on the negotiations. I think it was Circe."

"Why? And how do you know this?" I asked.

"I have photos," Marcel said.

"So you've been snooping on other people without their knowledge?" I asked.

"Like I said, some call it snooping, I call it intelligence gathering," Marcel said, his eyes flashing. He really was slippery.

"Who? And why didn't you share these with me before?" I asked.

"They're of Tony, though you might not recognize him in a few of the frames," Marcel said.

"What do you mean —" I asked, but Marcel disappeared in a blur of motion and came back seconds later with another stack of photos — this time of Circe's house on Moonbeam Lane. My heart dropped into my stomach.

"Go ahead, look through them. When you're finished, we can discuss who's really at fault here," Marcel said.

Like a moving picture book, I flipped from one photo to the next and couldn't believe what I was seeing. There was an eerie red tint to the photos thanks to the Blood Moon, making the bald man standing outside Circe's house that much more obvious. It was Tony Romano.

"You followed him that night?" I asked.

"Of course I did. After I got those photos of him inside Hypnotic Tonics after hours, I knew he was up to something and that it was only a matter of time before he gave me another bombshell," Marcel said. "Little did I know that's literally what he had in mind: firebombs. Keep looking."

I flipped to the next photo and squinted to make out what was going on inside it. In the same place where Tony had been standing in the last photo, there was now a man twice his size with a full head of hair and what looked to be a glass vial in one hand.

I gasped and dropped the photos, sending them fluttering down to the ground around me like snow.

"Tony killed Circe," I breathed, still unable to believe the words as they left my mouth.

"Exactly. He burned Circe's house down for calling off the negotiations. Based on what I've learned since then, he wasn't associated with the most savory people and I'm willing to bet he had a lot riding on whatever deal he was supposed to strike with the Council," Marcel said.

"Maybe some sort of windfall in order to pay back people he owed money to? Or some other perks in exchange for debt relief?" I asked. The image of all the cash sitting on Tony's desk at Pupperoni Pizza flashed through my mind, which made me doubt it was money he needed. But if not money, then what?

"I don't know. I still haven't been able to find the answer, but that's exactly what I've been doing these last few nights," Marcel said. "So when Hypnotic Tonics went up in flames yesterday, naturally my first inclination was to look into Tony Romano."

"Wait, back up, you still haven't told me why didn't you show me these photos the last time I was here," I said.

"I needed to know I could trust you first," Marcel said.

"Trust me?"

"Yes. I knew I needed help to bring Tony down, but I couldn't go showing these photos to just anyone. Obviously, I didn't want to go to the police with them either because, like I told you before, the werewolves are infamous for protecting their own," Marcel said, smiling.

Had I been wrong about him this whole time? While I thought he was stirring the pot for a salacious story for Grave Times, he'd actually been working two steps ahead of me to figure out why Tony killed Circe.

"Why didn't you just ask for my help then?"

"Like I said, I had to be sure I could trust you first. I know about the work you've done around here, but I was still leery," Marcel said.

"But you're not now?"

"No, not even a little bit," Marcel said, his smile widening. I didn't know how to take that, but I smiled back at him anyway.

"Good. Since we're sharing secrets here, did you know that Tony *and* Lorelei gave Hilda a loan to open Hypnotic Tonics?" I asked. Marcel's smile vanished.

"No," he said. "I mean, of course I knew about Lorelei's, but I didn't know Tony had a financial interest."

"So do you think Tony was the one behind the explosion at Hypnotic Tonics too?" I asked.

"Who else could it have been? The Council tried to pin it on Sage, but I never believed that. No one in their right mind would blow up their own store while they were still inside it. Lorelei gave Hilda money too, so it wouldn't make sense for her to torch the shop. There's no one but Tony who fits the bill," Marcel said.

"And if it's true that Hilda owed Tony money, we can only assume that Tony would've had access to pretty much anything he wanted in that store — including the ingredients to make Wild Fyre. Hilda and Sage would've had to give him anything he demanded because they owed him money they couldn't pay back," Marcel said.

"That's it! He was trying to destroy all the evidence," I said, comprehension dawning on me. "He couldn't trust Hilda and Sage not to rat him out. Outside of him, no one else besides those two would've had access to the formula or the ingredients to make Wild Fyre, and they were both in on selling him ingredients."

"Bingo. He needed to wipe the slate clean, remove all witnesses, and rid himself of the burden that was Hypnotic Tonics," Marcel said.

"Exactly, and based on the stacks of cash I saw in his office, I wouldn't be surprised in the slightest if the money he gave Hilda wasn't his to give," I said.

"Probably not, so when the loan sharks came calling for their money and Tony no longer had it, he saw one way out," Marcel said. "Killing Hilda and Sage would make sure his involvement in Circe's death never got out, and he could tell whoever he owed money to that he'd lost a ton of cash on a bad investment. They wouldn't be happy about it, but they'd understand and give him more time to come up with the money."

I had to admit, it was brilliant on Tony's behalf. I wouldn't have pegged him as being so smart — and had it not been for Marcel, I wouldn't have known any of it. Maybe I did need to start networking more with other reporters in town.

"The only problem is that Sage survived," I said. "And she swore it was Lorelei who had bombed Hypnotic Tonics."

"Of course she did. If she implicated Tony, she'd be in just as much trouble as he was because she probably provided the ingredients and made the Wild Fyre for him," Marcel said. "If Lorelei went down with all the blame, Sage would get out scot-free."

"She's the key to all this. She might not have committed the murder, but she signed her name to it and had to have known Tony's intentions," I said. Marcel nodded.

"Though to be fair to Sage, I don't think she had any idea what was going to happen last night," he said. "I think our friend Tony was trying to tie up the last loose ends."

"Which means he's still not finished," I said and dread swelled in my chest.

"Not until *all* the evidence goes up in smoke," Marcel said.

"He's going to try to kill Sage, isn't he?" I asked.

"What other choice does he have?" Marcel asked. "It's either that or let the truth come out and spend the rest of his life in prison — or worse when the loan sharks catch up to him."

"We have to stop him," I said. "The Council is holding Sage somewhere, but not even they can stop Wild Fyre."

"And that's assuming he isn't already there. Let's go," Marcel said as he reached for his camera, and I didn't bother arguing.

CHAPTER SIXTEEN

I POWERED down Fang Street with a stitch in my side. Marcel had run far ahead of me in a blur of motion because we assumed we'd look doubly suspicious walking through the Werewolves' Quarter together — a witch and a vampire did make odd company, even on a good day.

In stark contrast to the last time I'd been here with Beau, there were dozens of people out on the street. Maybe it was because it was after dark? Were the werewolves nocturnal too? I had no idea.

Regardless, most of them looked harmless, though they did stare at me like I was more than a little suspicious — who could blame them, they had to know who I was — but I tried to pay them no mind. The only thing I cared about was getting to Tony before he had the chance to do anything rash.

With my hands in my pockets, I strolled across the circular square toward the flashing light of Pupperoni Pizza. Surprisingly, it was the only light on in the place. Either Tony and Adriana had closed early, which seemed unlikely, or Tony was too busy plotting his next murder to be bothered running a pizza parlor.

Marcel said he was going to scope the place out from afar with his vampire vision and supercharged camera, but I wished now he hadn't. It wasn't like I could just run up to the front door with every werewolf on the street watching me. Granted, none of them were in wolf form so at least I didn't have that to worry about, but still, I felt like no matter what I did or where I went, at least a dozen pairs of eyes would be on me at all times.

But I didn't know what else to do, so I walked up the stairs of the restaurant, doing my best to look like an inconspicuous tourist who was curious if the restaurant was open. I pressed my face to the glass cutout in the door, which fogged as I breathed, but all I saw was blackness inside.

A chill ran down my spine. I couldn't say where Tony was, but he definitely wasn't in the restaurant.

"Zoe," a voice hissed from somewhere behind the restaurant and I jumped. Careful to make sure no one was paying to close attention to me, I went back down the stairs and rounded the corner of the building toward the woods behind it. Squinting against the darkness, I didn't see anything.

"Over here," the voice hissed and I took a few steps further into the woods. The glint of the moonlight on glass caught my eye and I breathed a sigh of relief when Marcel stepped forward and I realized it was his camera's lens that'd caught the light.

"Did you see anything?" he asked.

"Nothing. There's not a soul in there," I said.

"Yes, there is," Marcel said. Given that he had at least twice the range of vision I did, I had to take his word for it.

"There is?" I asked.

"The shades are drawn so I can't make it out with my eyes or with my camera, but there's definitely movement," Marcel said. "Whoever's inside doesn't want us to know anyone's home."

"What are we gonna do?" I asked. My first instinct was to call the police, but based on everything Marcel had told me about how they liked to protect their own, I highly doubted they'd show up — and even if they did, it might be too late by the time they got to the restaurant.

"What *can* we do?" Marcel asked.

"What if Tony's got Sage in there?" I asked. "We have to do *something*. Can you tell if it's one person or several inside?" I asked.

"No idea," Marcel said. "I even tried using the infrared lens on my camera but the shades are blocking it."

"Then I guess we'll just have to rely on the element of surprise," I said.

"What are you talking about?"

"Now's not the time to chicken out. We already know what Tony's capable of, and it's more than a little suspicious that the parlor is all closed up this early on a Wednesday night," I said. Truthfully, the last time I was inside there wasn't any business to speak of, so it was possible they'd just gone home early.

But as much as I wanted to believe it, I couldn't.

"So you're just going to sneak in there somehow and then do

what, exactly? Zoe, we're dealing with a murderer here," Marcel said.

"What else can we do? The police aren't going to be any help and anyone else we tell probably won't believe us," I said.

"True, but what happens if you break in there and no one's even in danger? Something tells me Tony's not going to just let that go, and based on what you've been through with the Council lately, I don't think you have any favors left to cash in with them," Marcel said.

He wasn't wrong, and it made me think of Grandma. I'd gone through so much trouble to get her into town, and she'd never forgive herself if I got hurt while she was here — and Raina would probably kick me out of Veilside forever if she found out.

But I couldn't leave Sage in there all alone with Tony.

"Here, take this," I said and handed him my phone from the pocket of my robes. The last thing I wanted was for it to ring while I was in the middle of breaking and entering.

"If I'm not back in ten to fifteen minutes, call the police," I said.

"What? What am I supposed to tell them if I do have to call?" I asked.

"Tell them there's a situation at Pupperoni Pizza they need to know about and that they should get over there as fast as possible unless they want another fire," I said. Now that Moon Grove had been through two of them, I had a feeling nothing would be as motivating to the police as the threat of another.

"Zoe, please, there's gotta be another way," Marcel begged.

"Unless you want to do it for me — and I don't imagine you want a close encounter with fire — there's not," I said. "Just stay out of sight and watch my back. Hopefully, this is all for nothing," I said, though I knew better than to believe it.

Even if I got into the restaurant and Tony wasn't there, whoever was could probably tell me where he'd gone. Best case scenario, it was Adriana hanging out in the restaurant alone cleaning up in the dark, totally unaware of her husband's plan.

I didn't want to think about the worst case scenario.

"And make sure you take plenty of pictures, we're going to need them," I said as I stepped away from Marcel. He hissed after me, but I paid him no mind as I crouched down and approached the back door of the restaurant. Luckily, a large dumpster parked beside it blocked me from anyone who might've been looking.

My heart hammering in my chest, I rested my ear against the cold metal door and strained to hear anything from inside. Nothing came, not even the sound of running water or the scrape of plate against plate being washed.

Fearing the worst, I wrapped my hand around the doorknob and gave it a twist. Amazingly, the door creaked open and I jumped back from it, every hair on my body standing straight up.

"Adriana?" I hissed into the darkness and I held my breath while I waited for an answer, but it never came. "Sage?" I asked, but still no answer.

Though I would've given anything to walk away, I knew I didn't have a choice. Besides Marcel, no one suspected Tony of anything, and if I didn't try to stop him, Lilith only knew what he might do — to Sage or to others.

After taking a series of deep breaths, I stepped over the threshold into the dark restaurant and froze, giving my eyes time to adjust. Despite the number of times I blinked, I still couldn't see a thing, until finally my eyes refocused and a kitchen appeared among the shadows. To the right, a giant industrial sink lined the wall, and to the left, a small set of three stairs led into the restaurant.

I lifted and placed my feet carefully, terrified of stepping on something and falling or making noise to alert anyone I was there — though they probably already knew from me hissing various names. I brought my hands up closer to my head to protect it, just in case something or someone decided to lunge out at me from the darkness and headed for the stairs.

I'd just reached the bottom when a muffled whimper sent my heart careening into my throat and I whirled around, nearly falling down the stairs.

"Who's there?" I hissed, squinting in the direction the whimper had come from. "Sage?" I called and a moan answered, drawn out and terrified. I followed it back into the kitchen, using my hands to guide me through the darkness. The sink was like a rail leading me toward the back right corner, and when I reached the end the moan came again.

I gasped when I looked down and saw Adriana sitting with her hands and legs tied together like a wild animal. A thick wad of what looked like medical gauze was shoved into her mouth, held in place by crudely-applied duct tape.

My hands trembling, I pulled the tape off and yanked the gauze out of her mouth.

"Zoe, oh, thank Gawd," Adriana sobbed.

"What's going on?" I whispered.

"It's Tony," Adriana said, clapping a hand over her mouth like it pained her too much to say the rest.

"Is he here?" I asked. Adriana nodded and jabbed a manicured, bejeweled finger through the darkness at the stairs.

"Did he do this to you?" I asked and Adriana sobbed.

"I don't know what's happening," she whispered, somewhere between choking and crying.

"Okay, okay, stay here and stay quiet," I said. My heart rate tripled as I crossed the kitchen again toward the stairs. At the foot, I strained to hear what I was about to walk into, and though I heard a muffled voice, I couldn't understand what it said — nor who'd said it.

Crouched down, I stepped up the stairs as slowly and quietly as possible, praying to Lilith or whoever was listening that the stairs didn't creak. At the top, a two-way metal door led into the heart of the restaurant, and I tried to visualize in my head where it might open.

I crept to the door, resting my back against the wall as I did so, and cursed the Council for taking my wand away. There probably wasn't much I could do with it anyway, but it would've made me feel somewhat more secure just to have *something* in my hand.

The person I'd heard spoke again, louder this time. It was definitely a male, but I couldn't make out who it was or what they'd said. Though every voice in my head screamed at me to do otherwise, I knew it was now or never. If Tony had Sage in the other room like I thought he did, even a few seconds could make all the difference.

I took a series of the deepest breaths I could manage and pushed myself up onto my feet using the wall. After counting to three several times and chickening out, I braced myself and charged through the swinging door, nearly tumbling to the ground on the other side.

It wasn't at all what I expected.

In the center of the restaurant, Tony sat in a rickety wooden chair, his arms tied behind his back with duct tape. Sage Snow stood over him, a glass vial in one hand with her other holding Tony's mouth open.

"No!" I shouted and Sage froze, the amber liquid inside the vial stopping at the lip.

"I guess today's your lucky day, isn't it?" Sage asked as she patted Tony's cheek. He seemed unable to speak. Had Sage cast some sort of silencing spell over him? And why was she trying to force-feed Tony a tonic?

"Somehow I knew you'd show up," Sage said.

She corked the vial and tucked it into her violet robes, the same ones she'd been wearing during the Council meeting earlier. Was her helplessness and hurt over Hilda's death all an act? And what other surprises did she have hiding in her robes?

"What are you doing?" I asked.

"What does it look like? Tying up loose ends," Sage said. She stepped around Tony and sat in his lap, forcing another moan out of him.

"I thought —"

"That things would be different in this room?" Sage interrupted. "I don't doubt you did. Honestly, I'm amazed you were able to put it all together, or at least, most of it."

"You killed Circe?" I asked. It didn't make sense. I'd seen the photos Marcel took of Tony turning into a wolf outside of Circe's house and there was no mistaking the green liquid in the vial in his hand as anything other than Wild Fyre.

"Not exactly," Sage said, still smiling.

"You either did or didn't," I said. Sage tsked at me and shook her head.

"No, I have my little pup here to thank for that," she said and tapped Tony on the chin. "I wasn't the one who started the fire."

"Why? What did she ever do to you?" I asked, anger and confusion bubbling at the back of my throat.

"The same thing you're doing now: asking too many questions," Sage said as she pushed herself out of Tony's lap to stand. I took a few steps backward, afraid of what she might do. Sage smirked at me.

"The simple answer is she knew too much," Sage said. "Thanks to Lorelei breathing down our necks at the shop, Circe got wind that Tony was spending a lot of time with Hilda and me. She found that a little too interesting to leave alone. At least Lorelei knew to keep her mouth shut, probably because she had something to lose too."

"Circe knew about Tony's loan to Hilda, didn't she?" I asked.

"Yes, unfortunately. One of Tony's little doggy friends ratted him out," Sage said.

"Doggy friends?"

"The mob, Zoe. You've got a good brain on your shoulders, use it," Sage snapped.

Wow. Though I'd heard the words come out of her mouth, and wondered about it myself, I still found it hard to believe there was really such a thing as a werewolf mafia. Moon Grove never failed to surprise me.

"Why would they tell Circe anything about that though? Wouldn't that open their ring up to more questions?" I asked.

"Mobsters will do anything to get their money back, and Tony wasn't the only werewolf with a relationship to the Council," Sage said with a shrug. Did that mean Tony had help from the mob in his negotiations with the Council for werewolf power too? It would make sense for the mob to want in on something like that.

Tony grumbled incoherently.

"So the money Tony gave you and Hilda wasn't his," I said.

"Sure wasn't," Sage said. "I wish I'd known that at the time, but when your back's against the wall and someone offers you a lifeline, you aren't exactly inclined to say no."

"Why did he give it to you then?" I asked.

"I'm tired of speaking for him," Sage sighed and whipped her wand out of her robes. I recoiled, convinced she was going to hex me to pieces, and she laughed.

"After our little chat at Mooney's I would've guessed all your time chasing killers made you fearless, but you're awfully jumpy tonight, Zoe," she said. She waved her wand at Tony and muttered a spell I couldn't hear.

"Zoe, don't listen to a word she says, she's full of—"

"Good ideas," Sage interrupted. "Tell her the truth, Tony. Don't make me silence you again," she said as she jabbed her wand tip into his chest. He cringed and whined.

"All right, fine. Look, I was deep in the hole with the restaurant," Tony said, which wasn't a surprise to me at all. "So I hit up some old friends I haven't talked to in a long time for help."

"You mean the mob," I said.

"Yeah, whatever, call it what you want," Tony said. "But they gave me more than I needed, way more. I wasn't going to refuse it, so I thought I'd stash the leftovers by—"

"Giving it to Hilda as a loan so you could keep making money off the initial amount and they'd never know," I whispered, my eyes wide.

"Now she's using her noggin!" Sage said, smiling, but it didn't bring me any comfort. I still didn't know what she planned to do.

"But then the mobster told Circe you'd stolen money from them, and she must've put two and two together. You were terrified word would get back to your friends that you'd duped them, so Circe had to go before she could report back," I said.

"I'm sorry, Zoe," Tony sobbed, but I didn't believe him or feel sorry for him. He'd gotten himself into this mess.

"If it makes you feel any better, I didn't want to hurt Circe. I tried to convince Tony it was a bad idea, but he was like a dog with a bone. When the Council announced the curfew and threw Tony out of the meeting, I knew he wouldn't let it go and I couldn't exactly tell him what to do."

"So he pressured you to make the Wild Fyre for him," I said. Sage nodded.

"I didn't really have a choice. We owed Tony a lot of money for his help, but there wasn't nearly enough coming in to pay him and Lorelei back," Sage said. "So we came up with an arrangement: I'd feed him as many tonics as he wanted until we were making enough to start paying him properly."

"Where did you get the formula for the Wild Fyre?"

"Tony's friends know a thing or two about getting their hands on illegal items, don't they, Tony?" Sage asked over her shoulder. Tony groaned and nodded.

"They bought it off some warlock months ago but thought it was fake," he said. "Least that's what they told me." Clearly, it wasn't.

"And they got ahold of another formula to stop a werewolf from changing under the full moon," Sage said.

"So the Blood Moon was the perfect setup," I said as I worked through it all. "No one would be out wandering around to see, and Tony wouldn't be suspicious if he was found out after the curfew."

"What a stroke of luck, right? We thought this time would be different thanks to the werewolves working with the Council, but the Council proved us all wrong and implemented a curfew anyway," Sage said. "But even with the perfect circumstances, Tony still messed everything up."

"How?"

"He got antsy and drank the anti-shifting tonic before it was finished fermenting," Sage said.

"So the effects didn't last long enough for him to carry out his plan to torch Circe's house. That probably explains why I tripped on this," I said as I reached into my robes for the vial stopper I'd been carrying since I found it.

Tony looked like the last of his dignity had fallen out of his rear. Sage whirled on him.

"What is that?" she snapped.

"I'm sorry, I dropped it," Tony said. "My hands were as big as plates and my claws were coming through so I could barely get the thing open. I didn't think it mattered, I figured it'd burn down with everything else," he continued and Sage looked livid.

"Incompetent *and* irresponsible, just great," she mumbled. "What else did you leave behind for her to find?"

"Did Hilda know you were planning to kill Circe when she

predicted there'd be death during the curfew?" I asked Tony, but Sage answered.

"Please, Hilda couldn't have predicted the rising sun," she laughed. "If it weren't for me covering for her, Hypnotic Tonics never would've opened and it definitely never would've made a dime."

"So Hilda wasn't involved at all?"

"No, she didn't have a clue," Sage said.

"Then why kill her too?" I asked.

"Funny you should ask because I was just about to force feed Tony a truth-telling tonic when you walked in," Sage said. It seemed far more confrontational than that to me, but I let it go. "Don't forget, Hilda and I were both in the building when it went ka-pooey. So, why'd you try to kill us, little doggy?"

Tony squirmed in his chair against the physical and magical bonds that held him in place until he exhausted himself.

"You were two-timing me, the both of you," Tony spat. "I gave you money that wasn't even mine and you were turning around and handing it to Lorelei."

"But Lorelei told me she wasn't getting paid either," I said. "So where was the money go—"

I cut myself off as the realization hit me like a werewolf's paw to the face. It was so obvious it hurt: Sage had been pocketing the money and playing everyone off on each other.

"The secret's out now," Sage said with a shrug. "You know, I guess it's true what they say about what happens when you lie with dogs: you always come up with fleas."

"And now you're here to make sure no one finds out. If Tony dies in a fire, the mob will stop coming after him — and after you," I said. Sage smiled and clapped.

"Well done!" she said.

Sage had pointed the blame for the bombing of Hypnotic Tonics at Lorelei during the Council meeting earlier — and lied to me personally about Lorelei being responsible — not because Lorelei had anything to do with it, but because Sage wanted to distract everyone long enough to be able to take care of Tony herself.

"You know, I had a feeling Tony might try something — he is a mobster, after all — so I kept an eye out and thank Lilith I did and that he's such a bumbling fool," Sage said. "I saw the klutz from the back window of the shop and barely had enough time to cast a protection spell on myself before he tossed the vial and the place exploded."

"You were lucky," Tony said, though he obviously wished she hadn't been.

"And it looks like I still am. Zoe showing up makes burning all the evidence that much easier," Sage said as she reached into her robes again. She pulled out a different vial from the one she'd been holding when I found her. My breath caught in my throat when I saw emerald flames swirling inside the glass.

"Wild Fyre," I breathed, bracing to run.

"Beautiful, isn't it?" Sage asked, her wide eyes filled with green as she held the vial up to admire its contents. Lorelei wasn't wrong; Sage really was a pyromaniac — and a murderer, even if her hands weren't the ones that'd committed the crime.

"You know there's nothing that can put it out, don't you? Not even magic can contain it once it starts," Sage said as she popped the golden stopper off the vial with her thumb. It rolled across the floor and stopped at my feet.

"But it has to start first," I said and without thinking, I threw my hands out in front of me, willing every ounce of magic in my blood to my fingertips. They tingled as psychic energy rocketed out of them in Sage's direction and collided with her, sending her tumbling backward into the wall — and the open vial of Wild Fyre into the air.

A whirl of sound and color flew past me and, screaming, I jumped in the direction of the vial, desperate to keep it from hitting the ground. With my eyes squeezed shut, I soared forward in slow motion for what felt like forever — but my fingers never met cool glass.

I thudded to the ground on my stomach, the wind knocked out of me. The vial fell just a few feet away from me, seconds from crashing into the floor and killing us all. Frantic, I thrust a hand out from under me with another desperate push of whatever powers I had…

… And the vial froze less than an inch from the ground as if it'd fallen on an invisible pillow.

Seconds later, the world around me came roaring back into focus. Flashing red and blue lights filled the restaurant, and Marcel was on top of Sage, pinning her to the floor. It took several seconds for my brain to catch up: despite his doubt, Marcel must've called the police like I'd told him.

"Zoe, are you okay?" Marcel shouted as leaned back to avoid Sage's flailing arms connecting with his face. Terrified, I pushed myself up onto my knees, grabbed the stopper that'd rolled away from me in the commotion, and plugged it back into the floating vial.

"I'm much better now," I sighed.

"Moon Grove Police Department, don't move!" Mueller shouted as he and Ewan Barrett stormed into the room, hands ready to draw their weapons.

"It's okay, we've got it under control!" I shouted back. Mueller seemed stunned to see me. He shook his head, his jowls flapping, and let go of the handle to his gun.

"Where there's smoke, there's Zoe Clarke," he said.

Despite the bad pun, I'd never been more happy to see him in my life.

CHAPTER SEVENTEEN

"YOU 'BOUT READY IN THERE, SUGAR?" Grandma called as she pounded on my bedroom door. Flora giggled from the living room.

"Just a minute!" I shouted back as I sized up the dress Grandma had insisted I buy from Zaria's earlier that afternoon. She wanted to take me and my friends out to a nice dinner, and she'd insisted that I look the part.

It was a form-fitting red dinner dress with a cute diagonal slice of frills across the front that ran from the middle of my chest all the way down to the trim. It wasn't something I'd normally wear, but Grandma swore it would be perfect.

"You done had fifteen minutes, so scootch your tushie!" Grandma said though I could tell from the sound of her voice that she'd already walked away in disgust.

"I knew inviting her over here while I got ready wasn't a good idea," I grumbled to Luna, who blinked her bright blue eyes at me like she was laughing.

"She's just as extra as I remembered her," Luna said while she groomed herself on my bed.

"I take it that means you didn't miss her?"

"Oh, of course I missed her," Luna said, one paw held out in front of her face while she decided where to lick next. "But it's easier to miss her when she's far away," she continued and I snorted.

"Eleanor Clarke in Moon Grove... I never thought I'd see the day," Luna said, shaking her head.

"Neither did I," I sighed.

"I almost wish I could come with you guys just to see her in action," Luna said, the beginnings of a smile appearing on her little kitty face. "Where are you going anyway?"

"I dunno, Raina made the reservations, but I'm sure there's really nothing stopping you from tagging along. Somehow I don't think of all things anyone in Moon Grove is going to object to a talking cat joining us for dinner," I said. "They've probably seen much stranger things."

"As hilarious as that all sounds, I think I'll pass. Besides, I still have a few episodes of As the Moon Turns to catch up on," Luna said.

"You're still watching those? Unbelievable," I laughed.

"Hey, what else am I supposed to do while you and Flora are out gallivanting around the town?" Luna asked.

"You mean other than getting up and going to an office every day for a paycheck?"

"Sounds horrible, not interested," Luna said.

Grandma pounded on the door again, making Luna jump.

"Lilith, I'd forgotten how persistent she can be," she sighed.

"Not me," I laughed.

"Hurry up or we're gonna be late, Sugar!" Grandma shouted. "Our reservation's for seven, I ain't about to miss it. I'll leave your tail here if I have to."

"All right, all right, I'm coming, relax," I said and stepped into my dress to tug it up over myself. I had no hope of zipping it on my own, so I went to the mirror across from my bed and fluffed my flaming-red curls so it didn't look like I'd literally gotten ready in less than twenty minutes. At least my makeup looked nice.

"It's a good combo, the dress and your hair," Luna said and I couldn't believe my ears. She rarely paid compliments.

"Did I hear that correctly? Did you actually just tell me something looked good on me?" I asked.

"Don't get used to it," Luna said. "Now get out there before Elle has an aneurysm."

"Fine," I said and flung the door open. Grandma sat in a midnight blue gown on the couch next to Flora. She stared at me with wide eyes and let out a squeal.

"Oh my Lord, it's perfect, Zoe! You look amazin'!" she shouted as she bolted up and dashed to clutch my shoulders. She turned me from side to side to take it all in. "I love what you did with your eyeshadow. The red smokey eye with the gold sparkles is really gonna pop."

"Thanks," I said, blushing though I didn't know why.

"Here, turn around and let me button ya up," Grandma said and spun me like a top. She yanked the zipper up my back in one easy motion and turned me back to face her. Tears were in her eyes.

"What's wrong?"

"Ain't nothin' wrong, I'm just so proud of you," Grandma said and threw her arms around me.

"Be careful, you're gonna ruin your makeup," I laughed as I hugged her back.

"Oh, who gives a hoot?" Grandma asked, holding me at arms' length to take another admiring look at me. "Isn't she gorgeous, Flora?"

"She always is," Flora said, smiling, and my cheeks stung. That was saying something coming from her. In her pearl-colored gown with her flowing hair dangling in curls from a sparkling tiara, she looked like a princess straight of a, well, fairy tale.

"All right, are we ready or are we ready?" Grandma asked.

"Ready as I'll ever be," I sighed and slipped into my matching ruby heels. Grandma escorted me outside, my arm linked in hers, and as the bright light of the moon bathed us I couldn't believe I was walking through Moon Grove with her — and how right it felt to have her there. My face hurt from smiling.

"Which way, y'all?" Grandma asked when we got to the end of the pathway leading to Flora's front door.

"Good question, I dunno where we're going," I said.

"You've been there before, Zoe, though you might not remember it. It's called The Root," Flora said and I laughed.

"Oh, I remember it all right," I said. It was the restaurant I'd run out of the last time Flora and I went on a double date with Ewan and Beau.

"My Lord, your wings are so beautiful in the moonlight, Flora," Grandma said.

"Thank you," Flora said and blushed as she fluttered them. They shimmered like light through a crystal. "They won't be the last ones you see tonight, Mrs. Clarke."

"Please, darlin', call me Elle," Grandma said and my eyes went wide. She only asked people she really liked to call her that, so that must've meant Flora was okay in her book. It put a smile on my face.

"Okay, then follow me, Elle," Flora said.

We headed east down Swiftsage into the Fairy's Quarter of Moon Grove and once more its trademark luscious, vibrant, and magical flowers surrounded us, their buds following us as we passed like the eyes of the Mona Lisa.

"Are they alive?" Grandma whispered and I chuckled.

"Of course, they're plants," Flora said and reached out to touch the rich pink petal of the nearest flower. When her fingertip made contact, the plant swooned and its vine wrapped around Flora's arm like a snake.

"Are they dangerous?" Grandma asked.

"Only if you treat them poorly," Flora said. She stroked the petal like she might a pet, and the vine released her. "Come on, we don't want to be late."

Three blocks further down, we stopped outside of an unimpressive building that looked more like a cottage in a children's story than a restaurant, but a wooden sign out front labeled it as "The Root Vegetarian Cuisine" in a twisted, tangled ivy font.

"Here we are," Flora said and gestured for us to go ahead. I took the charge, my arm still linked in Grandma's, and led us inside. I spotted Beau immediately in the middle of a long picnic-style wooden table. Raina sat a few seats down from him and Mallory and Ewan sat across.

Beau wore a powder-blue dress shirt under a navy blazer. A beautiful red flower peeked out from his chest pocket. He smiled and stood to wave us over. Grandma was about to meet my golden retriever shifter of a boyfriend for the first time and my heart hammered in my chest at the thought.

"Wow, you weren't kiddin', Sugar, he's a looker," Grandma said and I snorted as my face burned. I walked her over to Beau, my throat so dry it hurt to breathe.

"Beau, this is my Grandma Eleanor," I introduced her. "Grandma, this is my boyfriend, Beau Duncan."

Grandma extended her hand for him to shake and, always the perfect gentleman, Beau scooped her hand in his and placed a kiss on the back. Grandma fanned herself.

"You better watch it, boy, I ain't been treated like that by a man in a long time," Grandma said and I almost died of embarrassment right then and there, but Beau laughed.

"I'm so glad to finally meet you, Mrs. Clarke," he said.

"Call me Elle, and that goes for all y'all," Grandma said, waving a finger across the table. "I know we ain't all met yet, but if Zoe likes ya, yer family. Understood?"

Everyone nodded and Beau helped Grandma sit down in one of the two empty chairs between him and Raina.

I sat next to Grandma with Beau on my right. Raina beamed at us and leaned over to give Grandma a hug while Beau slipped his arm around my shoulders and pecked a kiss on my cheek. If I wasn't already wearing red makeup, my blushing could've passed for it.

"This is for you," Beau said as he reached for the flower in his blazer pocket. He tucked my hair behind one ear and rested the flower on top.

"How did you know I was wearing red tonight?" I asked.

"I might've had a little family help," Beau said with a wink. I faced Grandma and narrowed my eyes at her.

"Now Zoe, what have I told you about makin' that lemon-suckin' face?" Grandma asked.

"It's gonna get stuck that way," we said together and everyone laughed.

"This was a great idea, Raina, thank you for organizing it," I said. Raina waved me away, her deep purple robes flashing in the soft light.

"It's my pleasure, dear," Raina said. "You've now solved two murders in my family, so I think it's the least I can do to repay you."

It was supposed to be a joke, and a lighthearted one at that, but my heart fell at the mention of Circe.

"I wish she was here with us," I said.

"Who says she isn't?" Mallory asked from across the table. She'd tamed her wild hair by turning it into a long braid that trailed down her back and her shamrock-green dress suited her perfectly. I had no idea she could clean up so well.

"I didn't think you believed in that sort of stuff," I said.

"Zoe, I dunno if you've noticed, but we're witches. If you of all people can learn how to cast a spell, truly, anything's possible," I said and the table laughed again.

"Very funny," I said. "But I can't even do that right now."

"Maybe not for much longer," Raina said, her eyes twinkling. My heart raced.

"Does that mean what I think it means?" I asked.

"We'll see tomorrow morning, won't we?" Raina asked.

"Yeah, I guess so. I'm still surprised the Council decided to hold a public hearing for Sage," I said.

"What other choice did they have?" Ewan asked, both his elbows on the table. "She admitted to playing a role in the murders and she lied to the Council in front of pretty much the whole town. I don't doubt they're going to try to make an example out of her and probably Tony too."

"As they should," Raina said. "Moon Grove needs to know we won't allow this."

"Here, here. And to think I was working on a school project with her all along," Mallory muttered.

"Hey, what do y'all say we order up a rounda drinks before we get too deep in the weeds?" Grandma interrupted.

"Are you buying?" I asked.

"Nope, I ain't go no currency so I guess you're on the hook, Sugar," Grandma said and everyone laughed. She seemed to fit right in — with witches, fairies, werewolves, everyone — and it occurred to me that at some point she still had to go back to Lumberton, as much as I didn't want her to leave.

"Lookie there, perfect timin'," Grandma said as the same waiter we'd had last time I was at The Root appeared, his white-blond hair shining like fresh snow in the light.

"Good evening, everyone. I'm Sage, I'll be your waiter this evening," the fairy said and Mallory whirled in her seat to look at him.

"Relax, Mal, it's not the same Sage," I laughed.

"You're lucky, I was about to curse you to spell and back," Mallory said.

"Calm down there, killer," I said.

"Did I hear correctly that you're interested in some drinks?" Sage asked.

"You bet your purty lil' head we are," Grandma said. "Whaddya got? We need somethin' fun."

"I'm glad you asked. Our special this evening is a homemade favorite called the Fairy Godmother," Sage said and I laughed as I rested my hand on Grandma's — she was more like my Fairy Grandmother, but I thought of her the same way. How fortuitous.

"How'd it get that name?" I asked.

"It's an old family recipe passed down among the owner's family," Sage said.

"What's in 'em?" Grandma asked.

"A little bit of everything," Sage said.

"Sounds downright tasty. Bring us a round, would ya?" Grandma asked.

"Certainly, though I must warn you they're made with magic so you should be careful," Sage said.

"Ain't everything in this town? We ain't scared, let's have at it," Grandma said. Sage nodded and disappeared back into the kitchen.

"So, Elle, what are your plans now that you're almost as much of a celebrity around here as Zoe?" Ewan asked.

"That's a darn good question, and one I been thinkin' about since

I got here," Grandma said. "I got a farm that needs tendin' back home, but I ain't in no hurry to do it."

"Can't say I blame you. I can't imagine taking care of a farm without magic," Mallory said.

"It's hard work, that's for sure, but it ain't all bad," Grandma said. "But it's been awful quiet and lonely around there since Zoe came here."

"Have you thought about hiring someone to help you with it?" I asked.

"You kiddin' me? Your grandfather would come back to haunt me for the rest of my life if I tried," Grandma said and we laughed.

"Then what are you gonna do?"

"Well, like I said, I been thinkin' about it and I was wonderin' if maybe I could just, I dunno, stay here," Grandma said with a shrug and my heart skipped a beat.

"What? Are you serious?" I asked.

"Yeah, why the heck not, right? That farm ain't been nothing but a bee in my bonnet for years anyway," Grandma said.

"But you love it and it's been in our family for years," I said.

"That's true, but honestly, Sugar, I don't think I can keep up with it no more. It's too much for me," Grandma said. "Besides, after all I've learned about our family since comin' here, there ain't much about our family history that ain't bullhockey no way."

She had a point. If my mother was magical and if she and my father were still alive out in the world somewhere, who was to say that the story about how the Clarke family farm had passed down to Grandma wasn't true?

"I think that's an excellent idea," Raina said. "It would certainly help us speed up our research into your family's history, Zoe."

"I doubt the Council would ever allow it. They didn't even want you here for a visit," I said.

"I think they might be willing to reconsider now, dear," Raina said. "You and your grandmother were never a danger to Moon Grove and I think they see that quite plainly."

"She's right," Grandma said, beaming as she wrapped an arm around me. "You're gonna put the police outta work at this rate."

"I dunno about all that," I laughed.

"Maybe you could petition the Council again tomorrow? It would be a perfect opportunity," Flora suggested.

"Yeah, I guess I could, but where would you stay if they said yes, Gram? We don't have room for you at Flora's, and what would you do with the farm?" I asked.

"Sell it, I reckon. There ain't no reason to keep it around," Grandma said.

"You're more than welcome to stay with me until you find other arrangements, Eleanor," Raina said. "I've more than enjoyed your company."

"Aw, shucks," Grandma said. "Thanks, Raina, that's awful kind of you."

"Are you sure about this? It's not gonna be an easy transition," I said.

"If you can do it, I reckon I can too. And you bet your booty I'm sure. Your life's here now and I wanna be a part of it," Grandma said. I almost started crying as she pulled me into a hug.

Grandma might not have to leave after all. It was the best news I'd gotten in weeks.

Sage returned holding a massive tray on one shoulder loaded with seven drinks. He set the tray down on the end of the table and passed a glass to each of us. The liquid inside was a royal blue swirled with gold streaks and the straws dipped into it was adorned with a pair of fairy wings.

"Enjoy," Sage said. "I'll be back to take your order in a few moments."

"This looks fancy as all get out," Grandma said as she held her glass up to admire it. "All right, since I ordered 'em I guess I'll be the guinea pig and give it a shot first."

She took a healthy swig from the straw and her face puckered. She swallowed and made a weird noise.

"Wow, that lil' bugger's got some kick to it," she said and the whole table laughed. "But the taste is real nice."

I popped my straw into my mouth and took a small sip. Grandma wasn't kidding, it was strong, but the aftertaste was sweet and delicious. It tasted like cotton candy.

"A few of these and maybe I'll be makin' things float with the best of 'em," Grandma said as she took another drink. "Here, maybe I'll give it the ol' college try now."

Grandma pointed her hand at Mallory's shamrock-green clutch she'd left on the table beside her and made a show of squeezing her eyes shut like she was spending all her energy to lift the bag.

And it jumped across the table into her hands. A collective gasp tore across the table and I couldn't believe what I'd seen. Had Grandma really made the bag move?

"All right, very funny. Which one of y'all smartie pants did that?" Grandma asked as she dropped the bag back on the table like it'd burned her. I wondered the same thing, but from the stunned looks on everyone's faces, I knew no one had moved the bag for her.

"No way, there ain't no way I did that," Grandma said.

"I think you did, Gram," I said, breathless. Raina was smiling so broadly I thought she might burst with excitement.

"Aw, hell's spells, you mean I might be a Pagan sorcerer too? I guess I didn't pack enough of my crosses after all," Grandma said, and though I roared laughing along with everyone else, I could barely contain my excitement.

CHAPTER EIGHTEEN

THE ELEVEN REMAINING members of the Moon Grove Council stared down at me from high-backed chairs — Lorelei not among them — but with Grandma's hand in mine, I wasn't nervous in the slightest.

I glanced over at Tony and Sage, who were sitting far down the row to my right, their hands and feet magically bound so they couldn't run — not that they would've gotten far if they'd tried anyway.

Sage looked thoroughly bored, but Tony seemed like he couldn't sit still, constantly glancing over his shoulder. Being hunted by the mob will do that to a person, I guess.

The town hall was packed with people who'd come to see the two of them get their comeuppance, and I didn't blame a single one of them. After all the stress and violence Sage and Tony had put them through, it was the least they deserved in reward.

Head Warlock Heath Highmore brought the room to attention with his gavel.

"Chief Mueller, please bring the accused forward," Heath said, his voice commanding.

I hadn't noticed Mueller leaning against the far wall with Ewan until Heath said his name. Without a word, he and Ewan helped Sage and Tony out of their chairs and walked them to the center of the room. It was so quick I could've been imagining it, but when Mueller turned to walk back to his position, I swore I saw him wink at me.

Of all the friends I'd made in Moon Grove, I'd never considered Mueller one of them — but maybe I was wrong about him too.

"Ms. Snow, Mr. Romano, I won't waste any time with pleasantries. The two of you stand before us accused of murder and conspiracy to murder," Heath said. "The damage you've done to this community is in many ways irreparable."

"I'm sorry, I'm so sorry," Tony whimpered, but Heath ignored him.

"These are serious crimes that cannot go unpunished," Heath said. He waved his wand and another appeared. Based on the panicked look on Sage's face, it could only have been hers.

"Prior to calling this hearing, the Council discussed what an appropriate punishment might be," Heath said. Sage's wand drifted down and Heath stood to take it between both of his hands. He flexed it gently.

"No, please, I—" Sage begged. It was the first time I could ever remember seeing her afraid.

"Those who would use magic to murder — or to conspire to murder — cannot be trusted with its wonder," Heath said. "Sage Snow, you are hereby banned from practicing magic ever again. Your time at Veilside is finished. I suggest you find a new profession."

Heath raised Sage's wand and snapped it in half like a toothpick. Sage howled and when I turned to look at Grandma, she was smiling. After what she'd survived thanks to Sage and Tony, I understood. Though I took no delight in Sage's punishment, it was a relief to know she'd never threaten or hurt anyone again.

"Let this be a lesson for all in attendance. We as a community must learn to live in harmony. We will not tolerate the abuse of magic, Moon Grove, or its residents," Heath said as he looked out at the rows of people who'd come to see him do exactly this.

For the first time, I understood why he'd been elected Head Warlock — he was a true leader and I had more respect for him than I'd ever had at that moment.

"And you, Mr. Romano," Heath continued, glaring at Tony. "You murdered not one but two of our sisters, one of whom sat on this very Council."

"I'm sorry," Tony said, barely more than a whisper. Heath seemed unmoved.

"Jailing is not sufficient for your crimes. You are hereby banished from Moon Grove," Heath said and the spirit draining out of Tony was so palpable I felt it in my gut. "After the hearing, Chief Mueller and Officer Barrett will escort you out through the town gates and we will see to it that you are never allowed to return."

Tony's mouth opened and closed like a fish out of water.

"See them out, please, Chief Mueller," Heath said. Mueller seized Tony by the arm and hauled him off, disgusted. I could only imagine how awful it must've been for the Chief of Police to punish a fellow werewolf for something as awful as this.

Heath turned his focus to me and though I hadn't been nervous before, it seized me now.

"Moving on. Hello again, Ms. Clarke," Heath said, his demeanor changed on a dime. "We really need to stop getting to know each other like this," he continued, his eyes twinkling, and I laughed.

"Agreed," I said.

"I see you've brought a guest today," Heath said.

"I did," I said, squeezing Grandma's hand. Though she smiled at me, she seemed flustered.

"Welcome back, Mrs. Clarke," Heath said to her. "I hope we get off to a better start this time around."

"You 'n me both," Grandma said.

Her palm was slick with sweat against mine. Maybe I should've been as worried as she was, but somehow I didn't have it in me. All my friends sat in the row of chairs behind me — Beau, Mallory, Raina, Flora, and Marcel — unlike the first time I'd sat to request something from the Council.

Raina rested a hand on my shoulder and squeezed to encourage me. Once she told Heath and the rest of the Council about the magic Grandma had used the night before during dinner, there was no way they'd be able to refuse her request to stay.

Heath smiled.

"I assume you've come to ask something of us?" Heath asked.

"Yes," I said and stood, pulling Grandma up with me. "The last time I came before you, I asked you to allow my grandmother to visit me here in Moon Grove."

"I remember," Heath said, though he still wore a smile.

"At the time, I felt entitled to it. I thought that because of everything I've done — solving the murders of Harper Woods, Opal Cromwell, Delia Frost, and Seth Highmore, your grandson — the Council owed me a favor," I said.

Heath sat back in his chair and listened, and the rest of the Council remained speechless.

"But you said no and I didn't take it well. Instead of accepting your decision and trying again later, I went behind your backs and snuck my grandmother into town during one of the most dangerous nights of the year," I said.

Heath exchanged looks with Councilwoman Bloodworth, who sat closest to him.

"I don't regret it," I said and Heath's eyes went wide as the people behind me gasped or laughed or both. "I know, it sounds arrogant, but the truth is if I hadn't done it, I wouldn't have learned some incredible things about my family."

"Such as?" Heath asked.

"It turns out my grandmother and I have more in common than we knew," I said, smiling at Grandma. She returned it with a weak, nervous one of her own.

"Meaning what, exactly?"

"It seems Mrs. Clarke has latent magical abilities of her own," Raina said as she stepped out from behind me and strode to the front of the room. Heath stroked his chin.

"You're sure?"

"I saw it with my own eyes last night while I had dinner with Zoe and her friends," Raina said. "Show them, Eleanor."

Her hands trembling, Grandma removed her fingers from mine. I reached into the pocket of my robes and pulled out the vial stopper I'd found outside Circe's house the night she'd been killed.

"You can do it, Gram," I whispered and Grandma nodded. I tossed the stopper into the air and, just as planned, Grandma shot her hand out and stopped it right in front of her eyes.

Heath clapped, the only one to do so at first, until all of the Council joined in, followed by the attendees. Grandma pulled the stopper toward her and snatched it out of the air, beaming.

"Oh, come on now, it ain't no thang!" Grandma shouted over the applause, though I could tell she was eating up the attention.

When the cheering finally died down, I turned back to Heath with a smile.

"So, this time around, I've come to ask you for a favor, and hopefully I'm doing so while standing on much better ground," I said.

"Of course you are. If it weren't for you, we wouldn't have either of these two in custody, nor would we have any idea when or if the arson would stop," Heath said, nodding at Sage and Tony. Sage rolled her eyes.

"Now, what is it you'd like to ask us?"

"Can my grandmother move here?" I asked. No sense in sugar coating it. "I think she needs the magic study as much as I do."

"I see no problem with it, but far be it from me to speak for the entire Council," Heath said and my chest tightened. "We'll have to put it to a vote. All those in favor of permitting Eleanor Clarke to become our newest neighbor, raise your hands and say 'aye.'"

I held my breath while the Council reached for their wands. Heath raised his first, followed by Grace Magnus, and every other member, including Dawn Bloodworth.

"So it is done. Congratulations and welcome, Mrs. Clarke," Heath said and pounded his gavel against the sound block. Grandma ran and threw her arms around me, sobbing tears of joy.

"I can't believe this!" I shouted into her ear over the cheering from the attendees as Grandma squeezed me so hard I thought I might burst.

"Neither can I!" Grandma said.

"Congratulations, both of you," Raina said and wrapped her arms around both of us.

Heath banged his gavel several more times to quiet everyone.

"That brings us to our next point of discussion," Heath said when Grandma, Raina, and I had all retaken our seats. "It seems you're not the only one with some wrongs to right today, Zoe."

I had no idea what that was supposed to mean, but whatever it was, it sounded like a good thing.

"When we learned of what you'd done and how you'd put our community at risk — well-intentioned though you may have been — we snapped to make a judgment," Heath said. "In retrospect, the punishment didn't fit the crime."

Heath pushed his chair back from the raised dais and stood to rummage in his robes. A few seconds later, he pulled out a long, knotted stick — my wand. I swallowed hard. What was he going to do with it?

"To correct that, I'd like to return this to its rightful owner," Heath said. Using his own wand, he carried mine through the air into my hands. I wrapped all ten of my fingers around it and felt its power surging through my fingertips. Sparks showered from the tip.

"It seems it's happy to see you again too," Heath said, smiling.

"Does this mean…?" I asked.

"Yes. You're welcome to resume your classes at Veilside on Monday evening," Heath said and I was so happy I thought I might burst. Raina rubbed my shoulders from behind and I turned to see her beaming at me.

"I look forward to seeing what you learn to do with your magic, Zoe. I wasn't born with the gift of a specialty in Divination, but even I see amazing things in your future. Who knows, perhaps one day it'll be you who fills this seat," Heath said with a smile as he gestured at the empty Head Witch's chair beside him.

"Thank you," I said, barely able to speak. I couldn't imagine ever becoming Head Witch — it'd never occurred to me once — but then again, I'd never imagined I'd be living in a magical town with Grandma Elle beside me, either.

"Keep up the excellent work," Heath said. "Moon Grove is much richer with your presence."

"Thank you again, all of you," I said. Councilwoman Magnus applauded as she beamed at me and Councilwoman Bloodworth joined her though she didn't look nearly as enthusiastic about it. Maybe that was just her personality.

"You've earned it and more," Heath said. "Now, if you have no further questions or requests…?"

"No, that's all, thank you, thank you!" I said.

"Very well, then if there are no other issues to be addressed, this hearing is adjourned," Heath said. He waited a few moments for any last-minute concerns from the audience. When none came he banged his gavel one last time, its echo bouncing in my mind along with my buzzing thoughts and general disbelief.

I threw my arms around Grandma and let myself be dog-piled by all my friends as the Council left their seats and the town hall emptied around us.

Despite everything we'd been through, Grandma Elle was staying with me in Moon Grove for good — and that was all that mattered.

ABOUT THE AUTHOR

Lily Webb lives in the Pacific Northwest with her two cats, Hilda and Zelda, where she spends her time reading and writing all things paranormal. An aspiring witch herself, Lily's always been fascinated by the magical powers of the written word.

Connect with Lily:

fanmail@lilywebbmysteries.com

www.lilywebbmysteries.com

facebook.com/lilywebbmysteries

twitter.com/lilywebbmystery

instagram.com/lilywebbmysteries

pinterest.com/lilywebbmysteries

goodreads.com/lilywebbmysteries

bookbub.com/authors/lily-webb

amazon.com/author/lilywebb

Printed in Great Britain
by Amazon